"MOON SOUL, is a cozy sci-fi that is reflective, introspective, and fiercely intimate in its themes of exploration and rediscovery of the self while navigating a world of in-betweens."

–Ai Jiang

(Nebula, Locus, and Ignyte Award finalist, and author of *LINGHUN* and *I AM AI*)

"Luscombe hits again with his gorgeous prose. Moon Soul immediately and effortlessly connects with the heart and self, tapping into layers of raw feelings. This cozy yet deep sci-fi about a girl and her existentialism on a strange but beautiful world is an absolute, cathartic treat."

–Judy Liu

(Author of *The Vending Portal*)

"With thoughtful and evocative prose, this cozy sci-fi manages to capture the multifacets of human existence in a way that is equal parts complex, heartbreaking, and healing. This was such a thoroughly delightful reading experience."

–Jenni Sauer

(Author of the *War on Taras* trilogy)

"Introspective and cozy, Moon Soul is a scifi read that resonates with emotion and heart. Set against an alien backdrop, August's journey to found family and personal growth is at once familiar yet unique. It will pluck at heartstrings that have dared to question: Who am I? And deliver the answer in a gentle, enlightening way."

–E. A. Hendryx

(Author of *Suspended in the Stars*)

MOON SOUL

Nathaniel Luscombe

MOON SOUL
A Cozy Science Fantasy Novella

Paperback ISBN: 978-1-962337-90-8
Hardback ISBN: 978-1-962337-01-4

Published in Hackett, AR, USA by Dragon Bone Publishing™ 2024.

Edited by Effie Joe Stock
Cover Design/Art and Interior Formatting by Effie Joe Stock

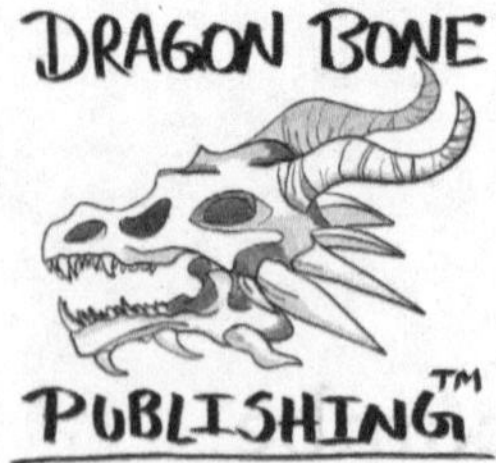

Dedicated to anyone feeling lost and alone in their twenties.

You are seen.

PLAYLIST

CHAPTER ONE: "Quitting" — Ian McConnell

CHAPTER TWO: "Simplex" — Kindiva

CHAPTER THREE: "The Call" — Mark Siegel, SVRCINA

CHAPTER FOUR: "Wandering in The Dark" — Ursine Vulpine, Annaca

CHAPTER FIVE: "Pink Moon" — AURORA

CHAPTER SIX: "Is This All There Is" — Hannah Storm

CHAPTER SEVEN: "Come Back To Life" — SKAAR

CHAPTER EIGHT: "Just Be" — Jamie Grace

CHAPTER NINE: "LOOK AT YOU NOW" — Gabriela Bee

CHAPTER TEN: "Universe" — Akshara

CHAPTER ELEVEN: "Perfect Movie Scene" — Moyka

CHAPTER TWELVE: "By the time you hear this" — Tuvaband

CHAPTER THIRTEEN: "Explosions of Grandeur" — Fleurie

CHAPTER FOURTEEN: "under the wave" — little luna

CHAPTER FIFTEEN: "Glowing Red" — Geographer

CHAPTER SIXTEEN: "Shake the Ground" — Dune Moss

CHAPTER SEVENTEEN: "Stargazing" — ARY

EPILOGUE: "Not Worried" — Nadiiife

Listen to the complete playlist on Spotify:
Moon Soul by Hecticreadinglife

A Cozy Science Fantasy Novella

MOON SOUL

Nathaniel Luscombe

Discontent comes so suddenly.

The pain of daily living is catching up to me. I've hit a point in my life where I can't ignore it. I wake up dreading my existence. I want to close my eyes and never open them again. It's hard to function this way. I go through the motions without understanding why I bother.

I guess I find comfort in filling that role. It's there to keep me on track. I want to be more than on track. I want to thrive. I want to be ... happy.

When I was seven, my father told me that he chose my name after a season on Earth. August. It's a long month, one that brings in the end of warmth and the beginning of cold. I couldn't help but take that to heart in a way they didn't intend: I began to view myself as an end.

It didn't help that they separated only a few months later, though it was less of a separation and more of an abandonment. My mother wanted to go back to her life in the desert. My father couldn't follow her there.

I can't help but think that the end is my only

destiny. Everyone dies, but is everyone only destined for death?

If so, we live a sad existence in a cruel universe.

Signed,

one who does not know who they are

ONE

I spend the night struggling to rid myself of emotions that are not my own. They're remnants from my day, little pieces I've picked up from the sand. It's exhausting trying to deal with them. How does one process something that does not belong to them?

I pace across my small room. On days like this my home feels like a cage, even though the outer walls are made of glass, opening to a breathtaking view of Argysi. Each time I pass, I touch the glass, trying to send some sort of feeling into my body—something that is my own.

The hardest part of absorbing other people's emotions is feeling things I have never felt. Today, I worked with two customers seeking memories of their parents. The intense love I felt conducting the emotions opened a black hole inside of me. I no longer have two loving parents and perhaps never did, making all my memories of love a sham. I'd been abandoned by both, even if one abandoned me because I told him I no longer needed him. It hurts nonetheless.

I crave love, but I want an organic form, not someone else's leftovers.

My eyes burn. I have been crying for hours, trying to drain the excess emotions. I'm sure there are red rims around both my eyes, and my cheeks feel crusted from the dried tears. Unable to do anything else, I settle against the glass and succumb to the overwhelming feeling of everything.

I feel the heartbeat of the Spire pounding around me. I'm on the ninety-sixth floor, only four floors from the top. The walls around me carry stories. I feel the gentle hum of the machinery within the Spire and the vicious winds rattling the glass, and beneath it all I hear the calming sound of music serenading my neighbor to sleep. I let the thrum fill me for a moment. In the Spire, we are only as good as our counterparts.

I wonder if anyone around me can feel my body shutting down.

◊◊◊

The blood doesn't come until I've left my apartment and gone to the roof. Every Spire has a publicly accessible roof; the ledge circling it is where the gardeners drop down from to work in the gardens that hang around the outside of the Spire. The Spire doesn't have rules against coming up here, just as it doesn't have many firm rules about anything, but it's an unspoken rule most people are fine heeding.

I stand as close to the edge as I dare and look out over the moon. Blood trickles out of my nose. I press my wrist against the flow, trying not to let it drip. I don't want anyone to wake up and find their windows splattered with blood. Despite my efforts, a few drops wrap around my skin and fall, only for the wind to splash them back in my face. I laugh, then grimace. The blood is warm on my skin.

The view of Argysi is the only thing keeping me calm. I hold a deep, aching love for this moon. It's the only aspect of life I enjoy, yet contact with it is why I'm up here. Why does it, with its beautiful, purple sand and sweet breeze, have to be the source of all my pain?

I walk to the spigot where the gardeners get their water and turn it on. A drain eagerly laps up the bloody water as I stick my arm, then my face, beneath the cold stream. I scrub at the blood. I can't tell if it has stopped flowing, or if the water is washing it away too quickly for me to notice. I breathe through my mouth, sucking in the fresh air.

I open the small shed sitting beside the spigot. On the inside, rows of harnesses hang on lines of hooks. I grab one and begin putting it on. The first time I did this, I'd struggled with figuring out how to adjust the straps. Now, it's almost second nature to pull it over my shoulders and clip the rest around my body and under my legs.

The gardeners use these to move up and down the tower. I often watch them from the ground. When they're near the top, they're nothing more than bouncing figures in the wind, possessing that wild freedom I crave.

Unlike the gardeners, I don't have the energy or skills to climb up and down the building. I just like to sit on the edge knowing that if I fall, the harness will catch me. I crouch down carefully, sliding my legs over the edge and letting them dangle. Pain dances across my soles. Just looking down makes my stomach feel funny. I embrace the discomfort. I'm here because of other people's extreme emotions. I think I need some of my own to counter them.

I take comfort in the fact that from this height, I can see Argysi's flaws. As with any moon, it's pockmarked and scarred from the space debris it shelters Oviun from. The green planet is hard to see at night when the dark colors fade into the universe, making it visible by the lack of stars in its place. It's an emptiness in the midst of everything else.

The universe above me, the moon below me, and me—stuck in the middle. I don't know who I am or who I should be. I am a being made from other people's feelings.

I don't think I can justify it any longer.

I'm going to quit my job.

TWO

The process of quitting is surprisingly easy. When I get back home, I put a notice on my website and send a notification via my comm to my current clients. Doing it early in the morning gives me peace. Not many people will see it right away. It might wake some of them, but I don't feel bad. I'm still carrying pieces of their grief inside me.

The sun is just beginning to kiss the horizon when I leave my apartment. I've thrown on a pair of pants and a loose shirt. I should be tired from not sleeping, but a mysterious energy runs through me instead. I make my way down the Spire, past fifty levels of housing, to the recreation center.

It's almost abandoned at this time. One man swims laps in the pool. He doesn't notice me when I come in, his face buried in the water. I watch him pass me with energetic strokes.

I head for the track and start running. It goes around the entire room, curving by the glass, then makes its way between other pieces of equipment. I'm glad the room is empty for now.

As the sun grows brighter, scheduled lights begin to turn on. Small groups of people enter the level. Some swim, some run, others gather in a corner and dance to quiet music. We're all training in our own ways, trying to keep our minds and bodies under control.

I haven't been down here in years. I used to come with my father, back when he still lived with me, and we would run together. That was after my mother left. I think we craved some sort of physical pain to make up for the chaos inside. Her departure put a cloud over everything I did. I still feel haunted by it.

Now, running feels like freedom. I'm winning back this territory on my own terms without my father at my side. Now that I've left my job, which has been slowly killing me for over a year now, I have so much time ahead of me. Time to explore, time to connect, time to relax.

I stop running when I feel like I'm going to collapse. It helped drain much of the built-up emotions that were boiling beneath my skin. I head for the shower stalls which line the wall near the elevator and stand under the freezing water.

My bitterness washes off with the sweat, vanishing down the drain, and I emerge as a new person.

◊◊◊

When I check my comm, a number of messages are waiting for me. I scroll through them slowly, taking time to pick them apart. They're questions I anticipated. People want to know why I'm quitting, what I'll be doing, if I'll be coming back. Some are wondering if I'm planning on leaving the Spire.

I edit my notice and change the word 'quit' to 'sabbatical'. Taking a sabbatical is common practice in the Spire, and I think more people will understand my need if I phrase it that way.

Doubt pools in me. I'm only twenty-two. Is it normal for people my age to feel this way?

It's not about the age, it's about the *need*.

I repeat this to myself as I throw the comm across the bed. After a couple minutes, I pick it up again. I need a new perspective on my situation. I open my calendar and check my schedule. My bi-weekly therapy appointment is set for tomorrow morning. I like to forget my appointments until they're about to happen. It doesn't leave me enough time to figure out a way to politely cancel.

Satisfied, I toss the comm aside again and lay back. Years have passed since I've given myself a day off. Years since I've looked at the ceiling and asked myself if I'm okay.

I don't know how to begin unwinding. It's something I've needed to do for so long. By putting it off, I've completely forgotten what it even means. I live a cyclical life. I go to work, I come home overwhelmed, I try to get rid of some of the weight dragging me down, and then I head to work the next day. Because I don't completely refresh during the night, I knew it would catch up with me eventually.

I just hadn't expected it to feel so sudden.

It doesn't help that I'm the only resident of this Spire who can do my job. It's not a necessary job, but it's one that many people seem to enjoy me doing. Without me, it wouldn't happen. A small worm of guilt wiggles in my stomach.

I wish I had someone else to talk to. Someone in my family. My father left for another Spire two years ago and my mother left over ten years before he did. My father is human, which is the reason I live in a Spire, but my mother is spyren.

It's because of her that I'm able to read memories in the sand—something all spyren can do. The gift is passed down from mother to child, a bond with the moon that roots our people here.

When the humans landed, they unbalanced the system. For spyren, leaving memories in the sand is an intimate thing. It's meant as a sign of trust for whoever finds it. When a spyren dies, their memories saturate the ground for the next generation.

Humans don't have such control over their emotions. The sand is overwhelmed with their memories, making it nearly impossible to process them properly. As a mixture of human and spyren, I am unable to intentionally leave memories, but I can read them. I have an unregulated connection to them to the point where I can't control their flow. Over the past five years, I've been earning my place in the Spire by reading memories for humans.

On calm mornings when sandstorms don't pose a threat, I lead them into the desert. I have to cover myself carefully, making sure I only connect with the sand when I'm ready. When I reach my hands into the sand, the entire world opens. I'm a conduit. The memories they seek travel through me and into them. I'm left with ghostly reminders, whether they be joy, grief, excitement, or fear.

Most people want sad memories; they're the ones with the most impact.

I carry more of this ghostly grief on my shoulders than I can bear. Somewhere along the way, I think I've forgotten where everyone else ends and I begin. I hope that by quitting, the emotions will slowly drain out of me, and I'll be able to live life in my own way. I want a simple life with simple pleasures. I ache to be able to exist in the way I see others exist, so carefree and excited. I am tired of waking up wishing I was dead.

Unwilling to make big decisions until I've talked it through with my therapist, I decide to spend the day at home. I'll enjoy the view and sleep until I can't sleep any longer. It's a start to whatever life holds for me next.

I begin by making myself a large breakfast. It's normally a small affair, something I grab on my way out the door, but this morning I stretch it out. I do it for pleasure as much as for need. Finding comfort in the little things is the only way I'll begin moving forward.

The doubt hit me again last night.

It was so heavy I could hardly breathe. I woke up thinking I was dying, but it was just panic flooding through my system.

I don't think there's much difference between panicking and dying.

I expect I will panic a lot less when I'm close to the end.

But right now, I'm jobless. My job is supposed to be my purpose. Without it, what am I?

People take sabbaticals all the time. I've just never heard why they take them, or what they do with them. I'm beginning to think I don't understand how life works.

Perhaps that's for the best. This is a fresh start, an opportunity to learn.

A strong part of me wants to cancel my sabbatical notice and begin working again. How comforting would it be to fall into that rhythm. Life is much easier without risks. Maybe not as rewarding, but a reward sounds like something I have to fight for.

I didn't bleed today. It's the first day in months that I haven't come home fighting the flow of blood. That restored a little faith in my non-plan.

Signed,

one who needs a guiding star

THREE

My journal is the mediator between me and my therapist Cora. It was her idea to fill the journal with my thoughts. Between sessions, I write down anything I need to release. I always circle the entries I want her to read. She's promised to not look at the others. There are things I've written that I'm scared of. My journal holds a true representation of everything I feel. It says things I don't have the courage to speak out loud.

I watch her read through the recent entries. Her lips move as my words pass silently through them. I can see what she's reading, can remember the words as they passed from my mind to the paper.

It only takes her a couple minutes to get through them. When she sets it down on her desk, it's with a level of reverence that acknowledges the heaviness of the words inside. She looks at me, smiling brightly. "So, you've decided to take a sabbatical?"

I nod, a little nervous. "I know I'm young, but it feels like the right time."

"It's a decision that takes a lot of maturity. I think you've made the right choice. Based on your experiences, you need a break. There's nothing wrong with that."

Something blooms inside me when she says that. The validation of knowing that I'm listening to my body correctly is not something I knew I was waiting for. I feel safer in my choices.

"Do you talk to many people entering their sabbaticals?" I ask.

"Of course I do. Most people are scared when entering one. They're worried they'll do it wrong, but there's no wrong way to do it. I just try to help people meet their needs. Tell me, what do you need?"

My mind goes blank. What I need is hard to differentiate from what I want. "I need to feel like myself again," I say, settling on a safe answer.

"What's making you feel like you're not yourself?"

My eyes dart around the room as I try to

find the right words. Speaking my thoughts out loud is harder than writing them on paper. "The fact that I'm starting to forget which emotions belong to me. Through my work, I've pulled on so many that I don't even know if any of them are my own." I wrap my arms around myself, feeling so small beneath my words. "In taking a break, I'm hoping to filter out everything that's not me."

"Sounds like you need a new job," she comments.

I falter, my mind racing. "I don't know how to do anything else."

"But you can learn." She leans forward on her desk, forcing me to look into her eyes. "No job is worth this much emotional distress. If you feel like you're losing yourself, you're in the wrong place."

"But I'm the only one who can do what I do."

"There it is then. That's the root of your problem, isn't it?" She sits back, satisfied. "Let me tell you something. Before humans came here, they didn't relive memories through the sand. You've offered something new, and people are going to take advantage of that, but you should never sacrifice yourself for the sake of other people's enjoyment."

"But what happens when I no longer have anything to offer the Spire?"

"You feel bad for taking when you're not giving?"

I nod.

The Spire works through a system that doesn't rely on money. People choose their contribution, whether it be making food, cleaning, working as a therapist, or any of the other various tasks. Together the five hundred citizens keep the Spire running. There are no rules about needing to contribute, but the shame of not contributing in such a giving society is enough to motivate people. It's a cycle that works very well. Sabbaticals are an understood break from work. A time to recuperate.

I feel selfish going on a break while continuing to benefit from other people's work.

"Don't make yourself earn a break. You're a hard worker and I've seen you push yourself beyond your breaking point. That's what got you here. It's not fair to you and it lowers the quality of your contribution."

It all makes sense when she says it, but I still feel weird about the whole situation. She seems to sense how lost I am. "Tell me about another goal. Maybe something that might seem ... easier?"

"I want to make friends?" The words come out as a question. Up until this point, it never occurred to me how badly I need friends. This morning at the recreation center, I became aware of just how alone I am. Everyone else seemed to have at least one partner working with them. I ran around the track on my own, a moon without an orbit.

I've never had time for friends before. Work forced me to take on strangers' emotions, leaving no energy or space for me to bond with someone outside of that.

Loneliness wells up inside me. Tears run along the edges of my eyes, and I wipe them away, furious. I've never cried like this during a session. Normally my tears stem from anger or exhaustion, but now I'm crying over something that feels pathetic.

My life is so empty.

Cora passes me a box of tissues. "Making friends is definitely an achievable goal. I think you'll find many people in the Spire looking to make friends."

Though she makes my problems feel so

easy to tackle, we both know it's easier said than done. I can't just *make* friends. I have to meet them first.

"I'm just worried people don't want to be friends with someone who's only half human." I look down at my hands, twisting them in my lap. "They don't know how to act around me or what to say. I'm not spyren enough for the desert and not human enough for the Spire. Where does that leave me?"

"Do you feel judged for being part spyren?"

"Not judged ... as much as watched. People are careful around me because they don't know how to treat me."

She taps her fingers on my journal. "That's not something you've really written about. At least not in the entries I've read. Do you feel that you're different from, say, me?"

I'm not sure how to answer. I've only known what it is to be between both worlds. All I want is to fit in. I want to exist in the Spire without feeling like an outsider. When I shrug, she takes a different approach.

"You'll find it's a very human experience to feel different. Many of my clients come here because they don't feel they fit in. Even the most human humans you could name probably feel like outsiders. Everyone seems to think they're the weirdest or the ugliest, not realizing that the people around them would never attach those labels to them."

"So, if I make friends, I'll begin to forget my differences?"

She ponders that for a moment. "I wouldn't put it that way. Differences are a good thing. Once you make friends, you'll realize that all your differences are what make you who you are. Individuality is an important component to a solid friendship."

The concept of having friends is difficult. I think of friends as sand running over rocks. They help remove the jagged edges and leave behind something smoother. I'm a very broken, jagged rock. I think I need someone who's willing to put up with me. Someone who understands that I don't know how friendships work.

Perhaps that's why the only person I talk to right now is a therapist.

Cora pushes the journal back to me. "I have a task for you to work on between our sessions. I want you to look into jobs around the Spire and see which ones might interest you. Even if you train for a few days and decide not to go back, I think it will be a good way for you to meet people and make some friends. You might even find something that you'd like to do more than your current job."

"Will people be okay with training me if I'm not even sure I'll be staying?"

"Of course! The Spire is built on shared experiences. People want to know that others care about their contributions. To pass on their skills is an honor."

With so many jobs in the Spire, the possibilities are endless. I need to find something to pour myself into. If I decide not to go back to my job, there has to be something calling my name. I don't want to end up in another bad situation.

"You look like you're overthinking it," she notes.

"There are so many options. It's a little daunting," I admit.

"Don't worry about it. You don't have to start training right away. Take some time to explore the Spire. Keep an eye on people and see how they work. I don't want you jumping into something you're not comfortable with."

I glance at the clock. Our session is coming to an end. While I feel better about my current choices, I now have so many more to make. But it's not Cora's job to make them for me. She's just here to help me think them through.

I take my journal, and stand. "Thank you for your help. I feel a lot better now."

"You're welcome. Please come back whenever you need to. You've got access to my calendar." She leads me to the door. It opens to a private hall where people wait for appointments they also might be scared about. I step through the silence, heading for the exit. Today is beginning to feel like the true start to my life. Much of my past has caused me pain, but I now hold my future in my hands.

FOUR

When the Spires were built, they were intended as resorts for the wealthy. This was over a hundred years ago, before either of my parents were even born. An earth-based company believed millions of dollars in profit could be made from a getaway on a small purple moon in an obscure corner of the universe, but the project failed due to low initial interest and the company removed what assets they could, leaving behind the Spires as empty husks. There was a collective purchase among several groups of people that was motivated by their longing for a haven. They were artists, lovers, and dreamers—the types of people who dared to look for a new way of life.

Now we remain untouched by the rest of the universe, uninvolved in the galaxy's politics. Supply ships arrive with the necessities that can't be made on Argysi, and they're divided between the Spires. They bring with them newcomers seeking change.

I dwell on what Cora said about finding my place beyond my work. As a child, I was fascinated by art. I've never tried to do it myself, due to the lack of time and the fear that everything I touch won't turn out right.

Today, I want to change that. I decide to go to the tenth floor of the Spire. It's a place my mother took me to a few times when I was younger. Completely overrun by artists, the entire floor is a beautiful display of talent and passion.

I stop on floor eleven to grab a drink and spot a man painting alone. He sits behind a table set up in front of the windows. Behind him, a layer of hanging gardens blow in the wind. The purple sky is brilliant and bright.

A heavy, sweet smell greets me as I approach. His table has been divided into two. On one side sits a single burner and a kettle of boiling water. On the other side lay his canvases and brushes.

He looks up as I near. "Good morning," he says. He's a man of soft features. His face is small, his curly black hair hiding much of it. His eyes are like the sky—infinite and full of contemplation.

I return the greeting, struggling not to stumble over my words. Even after years of working with strangers, I never grew comfortable with speaking to them. Several folded chairs lean against the glass behind him. He offers one to me and I take it, curious about his work. I sit and watch as he pours the hot water into three cups. The steam rising catches on his glasses, fogging up the edges of his lenses.

Pulling out several small bags of dry mixtures, he begins pouring them into cups. As he stirs, the water turns different colors. I spot a rich blue, a vibrant red, and a sickening green.

"What is that?" I ask.

"This is my paint." He pours a bit of the red one into a smaller cup and takes a sip. "It's also a drink. I'm trying to hit multiple senses with my art. It's pretty and it tastes good." He offers a small cup of the red drink. "Here, try some."

The cup is hot in my hands. I blow on the liquid, ripples spreading across the surface. When I drink, I'm surprised at the pleasantly sour taste. "That's amazing." I sit back and look around. "Why are you painting up here? Everyone else is on floor ten."

"I find it hard to focus with the noise. I work better in a quieter space." He dips the brush into the blue water. "Do you mind if I paint you?"

I don't. I settle into the chair and wait for him to give me instructions, but he dives into the painting without even changing my position. My eyes trace his movements. He's confident in his creation, using colors for my skin that I would never imagine. Slowly, a version of myself begins to stain the canvas.

I've never seen myself through the eyes of another. As he sculpts the shape of my face and pours on colors that turn into my eyes and mouth, my breath is taken away at the beauty of it all.

Throughout the process, he lets me try the different drinks. The green is very sweet; the blue almost tastes like nothing. They're good in their own ways, but the red remains my favorite.

When I tell him this, he adds more of it to the painting. My hair takes on a new color and my eyes become haunting, a fire burning within them. I blink, unsure of how I feel about this new depiction. It almost feels true to my soul, but in a way I haven't shared with anyone.

Each time I think he's done, he starts adding more details. An hour drifts by before he sets his brushes down. When he turns the canvas around, silence stretches between us. Upside down, the painting was beautiful, but it's nothing compared to what I see now. I can't take my eyes off this thing that was born in my likeness. Emotions have been painted on my skin for all to see. As they're something I tend to hide, it's a terrifying, yet freeing notion.

"Wow," I finally whisper.

I hear voices behind me and twist around. A small crowd of spectators has gathered behind me. They compare my face to the painting. I feel uncomfortable. I don't know when they arrived, only that they bore witness to something that felt very intimate to me.

The painter catches my eye and seems to notice fear creeping in. "This dries very quickly. The layers are thin. Take it. I want you to keep it." He pushes it across the table and into my hands.

The crowd is pressing closer. A few of them want their own paintings, others want to taste the drinks. I slide out of the chair and stumble away from the table, holding the painting carefully. I'm too far away when I realize I never got his name. I turn, debating on going back to ask, but the crowd has grown dense.

His work felt like a secret when I first sat down, a moment we shared together. Selfishly, I want his work to remain between us, but I know what the crowd's attention must mean to him as an artist. I hurry back to my apartment, shame spreading through me.

◊◊◊

I hang the painting above my bed. Over the years, I've tried to fill my walls with art. I've wandered through displays many times, considering the different styles, struggling to find something that spoke to me. Nothing impacted me as much as this image of my own face. Some of the color ran while it dried, causing a little bleeding around the edges, but the streaks remind me of teardrops.

I sit on my bed and stare into the eyes looking back at me. I feel they hold a truth in them that I have never been able to see. It is a frightening thing, seeing myself in the way a total stranger saw me.

I wish I could live without being perceived. I am very shy when it comes to my body. In a world where all sorts of surgeries are available, my pale blue skin hardly stands out. Still, it's a connection to a world beyond the Spire. A reminder that part of me belongs to the moon.

I don't think I can find a job within the

walls of the Spire. To honor both halves of me, I need to do something that takes me outside. Only one other job goes out there regularly.

The hanging gardens.

A shiver runs through my stomach. As much as I love going to the roof and putting on their harnesses, I've never considered trying to work with them.

I do a little research and find the people who run garden shifts. I reach out to them, asking for an opportunity to train. I don't mention my sabbatical or my previous job. This is a chance for something beyond that.

When I started my sabbatical, I didn't consider the fact that I wasn't required to do my job. I'd felt a heavy expectation to consistently fill the role. But just because a man can sing, doesn't mean he must always be a performer. Talent brings about opportunity, but it doesn't determine destiny.

That is the peace of life: knowing other options exist beyond the talents we're born with.

If I were to be cut in two, my body divided between human and spyren, I wonder which would make a bigger pile. I want to know the weight of my blood and the origin of my bone. I want to know which afterlife will claim me when I die.

Were my parents bound to separate due to their differences?

Does that mean I am bound to fight my own body? I don't have the ability to separate the two. They are both me, which means they must live in harmony.

Sand reading is passed from a parent to their child. I wonder if my children would have the ability and, if so, if it's my responsibility to bear children. I am part of a dying race. The spyren population continues to wane according to my mother. Seeing as I have never met another spyren, I don't find it hard to believe.

It doesn't feel fair, putting the responsibility of continuing a race on one person. I don't want children unless I find a very special someone. Someone I know will always stay by my side to help me raise my children. I will not raise another version of myself. I refuse to bring someone into this world, only to hand them loneliness and pain.

Perhaps that fear is what's holding me back.

Signed,

one who doesn't understand their body

FIVE

I rise before the sun, anxious anticipation thick in my veins.

A gardener named Lekka reached out last night and asked if I could join her early morning shift. Without the hanging gardens outside my own windows, I'd have never known the gardeners got up before the sun.

Instead of feeling tired, hyper energy courses through me. I head to the kitchen and make myself a cup of coffee. It's one of the things humans import on their ships. From what I've heard, coffee is one of the most desired substances throughout the planets populated by earthlings. Many other species have their own version of it. It seems it doesn't matter where one comes from: waking up is always a struggle.

I drink it dark to shake any last remnants of sleep out of me. After three days of not touching the sand, I feel so good it's frightening. I hold power over myself I've never felt before. As the coffee clears my mind, there's no twinges of pain, no massive headaches, no wanting to throw myself back into bed.

For once, I'm looking forward to starting work.

Lekka instructed me to meet her by the elevator. I check the time and head out. The hall is dark, dimly lit by two strips of yellow lights that pulse softly overhead. I walk past the doors of sleeping people and wait outside the elevator door. I want to be early and make a good impression.

As uncertainty builds, I push it down, unwilling to let it diminish the excitement I'm feeling. The elevator hums as the doors open, revealing a woman standing at the back. She looks me up and down, a smile on her face. "August?"

I nod, sudden intimidation flooding through me.

"Great. I'm Lekka. It's lovely to meet you." She holds out a hand. I step into the elevator and shake her hand. Her grip is firm, almost hurting the soft bones in my hand. "You have no idea how excited I am to have someone to work with. The morning shifts are so lonely. Too many thoughts and no one to share them with." She smiles.

I don't know what to make of her. Already, she seems so unlike anyone I've ever been around. Just by looking at her, I can tell she's tough and comfortable with herself. Her arms are muscular and toned from working outside; tattoos run down the right one. Half her head is shaved, and the longer part barely brushes her shoulder. I look away, unwilling to admit how much I've been staring.

I want to fit within my body as easily as she fits within hers. She inhabits every space, taking control of her image in a way that can only earn my respect.

The elevator lets us out onto the roof. She watches me, perhaps gauging how comfortable I am at these heights. I am much more familiar with this place than I let on.

"Today, I'm going to take it easy on you. We'll do some basic training, I'll show you the different plants, and you can ask me any questions you might have. I know you're just here to try this out, so I'll do my best to set up realistic expectations without scaring you away. Sound good?"

"Yeah." It sounds perfect. I'm so glad she's okay with me just trying this out. I don't want to start it and quit, but I might not be ready for commitment. "How long have you been gardening for?"

"Oh, probably ten or fifteen years now. I started when I was about your age, and I never looked back."

"You didn't get bored?"

She scoffs. "Gardening is pretty much the only thing I have to look forward to. For most people, plants are food. For me, they're much more than that. The plants are a symbol of my life's work. When they're healthy, it means I've been doing a good job."

I want this sort of passion for work. She's pouring herself into a place where she gets to see the benefits of her labor. Maybe that's what I've been missing.

She starts showing me around, pointing out the spigot, the storage space for the harnesses, and where they keep all the other supplies.

"I'm going to assume you've never worn a harness before." She holds one up, the metal pieces clinking together.

I'm a terrible liar. Heat instantly rushes to my face, and I look away from her. "I've ... worn them quite a few times," I admit.

"Yeah?"

"Sometimes I come up here to think. I like to put on a harness and sit on the edge."

She laughs. "I swear, you young kids do the dumbest stuff. As long as you're safe, I don't care. I'm glad you have a little experience. It makes my job easier." She tosses me a harness and I catch it.

We clip them on, moving the pieces over our shoulders, between our legs, and around our waists. The harnesses aren't too uncomfortable when I'm sitting on the edge, but I worry about the straps digging into me while I'm hanging. The material is hard, and I could see it leaving marks on my skin.

She hands me a small oxygen tank. It straps to my chest with a tube and mouthpiece that tucks into the top of the harness. The end of it sits close to my chin. The oxygen is a precaution against the infrequent sandstorms. When they reach their peak, they can overtake the Spires and any gardeners who happen to be outside, but the risk isn't high and the chances of being out during one are slim. We also have small goggles to help when the wind is sharp.

She prepares some other things. Such as bottles of water and small tubs of gray gunk that she hooks to our waists. I don't ask questions yet.

I know she'll offer explanations when needed. The last thing she hands me is a pair of gloves. I pull them on, the tight fabric snapping to my skin.

We step up to the edge of the Spire. It was only a few nights ago that I sat here and decided to quit my job. I can't believe I'm already back, this time in a way I never expected.

Lekka leans over the edge and pulls up thick ropes. They spool out beneath the ledge, hanging inches away from the side of the Spire. Lekka takes the end of one and attaches it to the back of my harness. She tugs on it to make sure it holds, then takes a smaller rope and hooks it above the first one.

"There's a two-rope safety policy for the gardeners," she explains. "We have the policy even though we've never had a rope break. Usually, the dangerous accidents only happen to stupid people. If you're working with me, I expect you to be smart." While she speaks, she connects herself to a different set of ropes.

"Yes, Ma'am."

She smirks. "That's the spirit. Now follow my lead." She turns so her back is to Argysi. She's in her element. She pulls on her rope, keeping it tight. "The easiest way to work is to pretend you're walking on the wall. It's always a good idea to stay close to it. Hang out too far and the wind will blow you around. I've had someone break their nose because they were free hanging in the strong winds. All it took was one big gust to pull them back and smash their face into the glass."

I grimace. The wind sounds malicious beneath us, whistling as it tears around the Spire.

"Don't worry about the wind. It's easy to work with once you get your footing. Just follow my lead."

I step onto the lip of the edge and turn. Having my back to the fall feels wrong. I try not to let fear get the better of me, but my hands shake, and my heart starts racing.

"Sometimes I start my day with a free fall. It helps me loosen up and get rid of tension. Of course, I won't make you free fall on your first day ... or ever if you don't want to."

I sigh. Just hearing her say 'free-fall' is enough to make me second guess every choice that led me here.

"We start by tilting ourselves back. It's like changing gravity." She crouches, tightening her knees, and starts to lean back. I watch her for a moment to figure out her posture, then follow her lead.

The gravity pulls on me as soon as I start. I gasp, my knuckles turning white as I grip onto the rope. The effort strains the muscles in my hands. Without the gloves, it would tear through my skin. My feet shuffle slightly, moving from the top to the side, and suddenly I'm standing in a way I never have before.

I release a relieved laugh. This isn't so bad. Since I'm standing with my back to the ground, the distance doesn't seem to matter. I look up at the sky, full of stars and satellites. It's beginning to brighten, the first streaks of light pouring over the horizon. I'm so glad I'm working an early shift. Argysi is so beautiful and quiet at this time. There are small ladders in front of us that bridge the gap beneath the ledge. I grab onto one and hang, the harness pulling against my back. I feel safer holding onto something other than the rope.

"Okay, now practice taking some steps back. Our first garden starts about twenty feet down." Lekka shows me how she walks backwards. With the rope giving her tension, she's able to crouch and almost crawl down.

I take hold of the rope. My knees ache as I follow her. It's not hard to get the hang of it, I just put one foot behind the other, dropping lower and lower until Lekka stops. I look over my shoulder and see the gardens below us. They run in tracks beside our ropes, bringing us right beside them. I also see the ground. It's so far away, purple sand scattering in the wind. My breath catches.

"Stop focusing on the ground," Lekka warns.

I turn my focus back to the rope and take a deep breath. It's funny how this scares me so much, yet other people do this every day. *I* could be doing this every day.

Lekka guides us to a stop beside the gardens. She says the hanging ones are easier than the panels. I'm grateful we're starting here. I'm still trying to get used to the harness.

The hanging gardens are wide pots dangling from studs that extend at even intervals down the side of the Spire. They sway gently in the wind, the chains making hollow sounds. This first one has small sprouts breaking through the soil. A small lip around the edge of the pot keeps the plants protected from the wind.

"We have two types of gardens. The hanging gardens carry the more delicate plants. These are the ones we keep higher up where the sand can't reach." She moves her legs away from the wall, her full weight resting in the harness. It allows her to hang in front of the garden. Her rope is locked and won't move until she's ready to descend again.

I sense her waiting for me to follow her lead. I start letting my legs slide, but my body seizes, and I have to pull myself up. The thought of letting myself hang freely above the ground makes my heart want to plunge to my feet.

"Don't worry, everyone gets scared on their first trip." She reaches out a hand, offering it to me, but I can't let go of the rope. My grip is so unrelenting, I'm sure there's blood pooling beneath my gloves.

Her hand stays outstretched. She's not giving up.

Eventually, I manage to let one hand leave the rope, though a scream wells up within me, and I take her hand. She guides me away from the wall, my legs slipping until I lose touch and swing out. A startled yelp escapes my lips. It's instantly caught by the wind and Lekka doesn't react to it. My face burns with how childish I feel.

"We have time. Don't push yourself. Adjusting isn't always easy," Lekka says.

I nod, my eyes closed. I feel the distance

between me and the ground. It's so vast that I'm scared it's going to swallow me up. The wind has more power here and as it flows around me, my harness rocks.

"When I started working here, I found that keeping busy was a good way to forget where I was. If you're feeling up to it, you might discover the same thing." Lekka pulls out her bottle and starts spraying the soil. "I start the mornings off by watering the plants and checking them for any signs of disease."

Taking my bottle with shaking hands, I help her water the plants. We have to be careful. Some of the plants are so small they hardly poke through the dirt. We turn the leaves over, making sure they're all healthy. Lekka explains the risk of parasites and how the leaves sometimes tear during severe sandstorms. Before bad storms, all the gardeners come out to cover the pots with protective casings.

We've moved down several gardens when someone falls past us. I jump, almost dropping my water. Lekka leans back in her harness and laughs. She points up at the top. Other gardeners are gathering along the edge of the roof; some coming down like we did, others choosing to free fall.

"Why do we start earlier than them?" I ask.

She shrugs. "Sometimes I come with them, sometimes I come earlier. It depends on my mood. I wanted to get out early with you today so I could train you before the sun got too hot."

The sun is crawling up the sky. Vivid purple and red streaks fill the air above us, the stars beginning to vanish in the light. I'm experiencing the sunrise as if for the first time from a view I've never seen before. The sunrise seems more vibrant here than it does when I'm behind glass. I feel the warmth seeping across the moon, the air gradually losing its bitter edge.

We work our way through the hanging gardens, moving closer and closer to the sand as we go. It becomes easy enough that we start working on separate pots. I spray, I check for disease, and I move on to the next garden.

As I settle into the rhythm, I can't help but compare this to my previous job. I'm still immersed in the moon, but in a totally different way. Instead of digging through the sand for someone else's memories, I'm growing food through imported soil. Even the air up here feels different. It's exhilarating having a new frontier of Argysi to explore.

The wind beneath us kicks up sand. I keep checking, making sure it isn't climbing. The last thing I want is for sand to start hitting us. I wouldn't want to experience memories while in the harness. There's no telling how that would go.

Since the soil in the pots isn't from the moon, it holds no memories. I find it so interesting that our moon is the only heavenly body that holds memories in its ground. Dirt without memories feels wrong ... a good kind of wrong. I wish I could walk through the desert without worrying about the trauma building on its surface.

The hanging gardens end and we reach our first panel—a wall of dirt built directly into the side of the Spire. Lekka opens the tub of gray gunk and dips her hands into it. She explains that the gunk is what holds the panels together, while also distributing a nutrient in the soil. We have to work the gunk into the soil to ensure that the gardens don't collapse.

I knew a little about how the panels worked, but now that I'm actually doing it, I realize how much I take it for granted. It's a common sight for those inside to see the gardeners hanging outside the windows, but from out here we can only see our reflections. There's no telling who might be looking at us. There are so many jobs in the

Spire that people don't understand or take time to learn about. There are people like Lekka who are so passionate about their jobs and so in love with their way of life, yet they get overlooked. They want to tell people about their work; they just need to find the right audience.

This mentorship is what I've been missing out on. I never had someone able to train me for my job. There was no one to teach me of the risks of taking on too many memories. As with all jobs, I'm sure there's an art to reading memories. I've just lost all desire to look for it.

I bury my hands in the nutrient. When I pull them out, it makes a strange sucking sound. It's cold and sticks to my gloves. When I knead it into the soil, the dirt spreads over my hands. Lekka works beside me, giving me tips as we move along. The plants that grow in this are called tubercles. They don't look impressive from the surface. They're just little bundles of leaves that barely poke through the dirt, but underneath are large roots that spread and tangle around each other. The roots are what we harvest. As the base ingredient for most foods in the Spire, they can be made sweet or salty, mashed, or boiled, or even eaten raw.

I feel them growing as I work my way around them. I love this connection I have with the natural world.

It takes us ten minutes to finish the first panel. Once it's done, we push back a bit and spray the whole thing with water.

"I can't go much lower. I don't want to risk touching the sand." I look past my feet. A couple panels down, I can definitely see purple sand in the air. The winds only pull it so high, and I'll be fine working on the panel beneath us.

Lekka glances down. "I didn't think about that. If you do the one right below, I'll do the ones further down. You can wait for me once you're done."

That's how the rest of the shift goes. It takes me over twenty minutes to do one panel on my own. Lekka works her way through the remaining three at ten minutes a panel. When she comes back up and we begin our journey to the top, warmth floods through my chest.

I think I've found my happy place.

SIX

I stand by the glass and watch the gardeners do their work. It's nearing the afternoon now and the midday shift just dropped down. It's strange standing on this side of the glass when, hours before, I was on the other side. Already I miss the wind and the rhythm of the world beating in my bones. I miss the connection I felt, not only to my work but also to Lekka and the other gardeners.

With them, I was part of something. I was no longer working on my own, doing a job only I could do. The gardeners have a team and it's one I can be part of.

Lekka told me I can work with her every other day. She already sent me a schedule once she found out how excited I was. I check it out, not for the first time, looking at the day after tomorrow when I get to go back out.

It can't come soon enough.

Today is a regular day inside; people continue to work. I see a man walking from one indoor plant to the other, watering them and checking their leaves. He does what I do, just on a different scale.

The air is warm and hangs heavy with the smell of fresh food. I like to think of how the bakers use many ingredients from plants grown outside. If I continue to garden, I'll be a link in the chain that directly impacts people. It's a useful position, one I take pride in. Never have I felt this close to the Spire. It's like I've finally shifted into place and the world now fits together perfectly.

A woman washes the windows not far from me. She hums a tune to herself, a wide smile on her face. Her movements are quick and practiced and she leaves spotless glass in her wake. She's so good at her job, it's almost an art form in and of itself.

At tables close by, groups of people sit together. They eat their food, scroll on their comms, and talk to each other. A man sits in a chair all by himself and reads a book. A mother walks along the edge of the room with a stroller, her sleeping child inside.

It's the first time I've noticed this cycle so clearly. Between the people working, others are existing. They're taking their time and using it in a way that's beneficial to them. Most of them will be working later or have, like me, already put in a shift. Whatever they do, they take time to enjoy their day.

The guilt of taking a sabbatical has dissipated now that I'm working in the gardens. On the first night, when I thought of no one having access to the memories, I almost retracted my notice. But the world moves on. The Spire doesn't rely on one being. Even though no one else can read memories, they'll find other ways to connect with their past. The more I think about it, the more I believe it's not a bad thing for people to be present in the here and now. Memories are of the past and that's where they should stay.

◊◊◊

I settle on a bench on level thirty-three. The back of the bench rests on the sloped edge of Eden, a large installation that cuts through the center of ten floors. It's a glass structure with an artificial jungle blooming inside. The warped glass fits perfectly through holes in the floor.

When I was a child, I spent hours staring into it. Though none of the plants are real, they sway in a synthetic wind and the result is mesmerizing.

A dish of warm food sits on my lap. I poke at it with a fork, waiting for it to cool down. It's fried tubercles. I rarely eat them in this form, preferring to have them mashed or cooked within something else, but after gardening I want to try them in a form more true to their natural shape.

I stab through one with my fork and take a bite. It's an interesting flavor accompanied by an interesting texture. Not quite sweet, not quite salty. Plumes of steam rise around my face.

Someone sits beside me. I glance over and a smile creeps across my face. It's the artist from yesterday. He looks over and grins. "Hello again."

I swallow. "Hello."

"I painted you yesterday." He seems to think I've forgotten him. His face grows red, and he goes to move.

"Yes, I know." I smile. "I hung the painting up in my home. It's a beautiful piece. I'm very excited about it. Thank you again."

"Oh"—he's visibly relieved—"I'm glad to hear that. I meant to get your name before you left, but everything happened so fast, and you were gone so soon. I'm Alix."

"August."

Now that I take time to survey his face, he's younger than I thought, appearing close to my age. This makes our meeting even more exciting since I want to connect with people my age. Lekka is quite a few years older. While I have no doubt she'd make a great friend, I don't know if that's something she'd be interested in. Age can feel like a divide.

"I didn't mean to interrupt your meal. I just saw you and wanted to introduce myself before you disappeared again." He laughs and goes to stand up.

"Feel free to stay. I don't mind the company," I say nervously. I don't want him to leave, but I also don't want to appear needy. It has occurred to me that I don't know how to properly make friends.

He stops in the middle of standing and slowly sits back. I continue eating the tubercles while he watches the people walking past us. I run through possibilities for conversation in my mind. How come I have so much to say, yet nothing comes out when I need it to?

"Have you done any painting today?"

He shakes his head. "I had a shift at the

water treatment plant last night. I was just finishing breakfast when I saw you."

"Artist by day, water treatment maintenance by night." I look him over. He doesn't strike me as someone who would work in water treatment. Though I pictured him having a more interesting job, I don't judge him for it. Jobs aren't tied to who we are. They're the places we go to survive, yet they don't even brush the core of who we are.

"Yeah. I mean, it's a pretty easy job and it doesn't require a lot of interaction with other people."

"You don't like being around other people?"

He avoids my gaze, his eyes wandering everywhere but my face. "I like being around people once I've gotten to know them, but I find it hard to talk to strangers. Besides, I really do enjoy being alone. It's when I'm the most creative."

"There's nothing wrong with wanting some peace and quiet." I finish the last of my tubercles and set the plate aside. "I just did my first shift in the gardens this morning. I'm trying to learn a whole new job."

"What did you do before the gardens?"

I freeze for a moment. I'm used to people kind of knowing who I am. They can usually tell by looking at me that I'm not fully human, and their minds automatically make the link between me and the only spyren in this Spire. Once I speak about being spyren, I can never take it back. While I don't think he'll have a problem with it, my stomach flutters anxiously at not knowing.

"I was a sand reader."

He can't hide the moment of surprise, but his face shifts back to neutral quicker than I'm used to. "Oh, wow. I didn't realize you were ..." he trails off, suddenly unsure of himself.

"Yeah. I'm spyren."

"You know, while painting you yesterday I couldn't figure out why it felt different. My hands wanted to do things my eyes were having trouble actually seeing."

The artist's eye. I wonder if that's also how he managed to carve a hole in my soul with his painting. Every color on that canvas summed me up perfectly.

"I'm sorry. I hope I'm not making you uncomfortable. I came to Argysi not too long ago and I'm still adjusting to everything."

By everything, he means me and the concept of spyrens. So many species inhabit the universe, and many of them are like me—similar enough to humans that we can share our living spaces comfortably. It's not uncommon for humans to be unfamiliar with other species. Of all of us, they're the most widespread. They don't seem as deeply rooted to their home planets as the rest of us. I've never really had the chance to explain being spyren to someone who didn't grow up around them. The people I take on tours are usually long-time residents of Argysi.

"It's fine. I'm used to curiosity. I have it too. To be honest, I don't know a whole lot about the spyren. My mother was spyren and she left pretty early in my life ... so I grew up just like everyone else."

"Not like everyone else. You don't realize how special this moon is. Most places aren't this kind." His expression dims. "I come from a dying planet. The people there have a heaviness I can't describe. It's nothing like you've got here."

I can't imagine growing up in that sort of environment. The Spires have sheltered me from the harshness of the universe. Argysi is a peaceful place, one embraced by a certain culture.

I am not keen on experiencing the world beyond it.

"I want you to teach me how to paint. Or ... I just want to paint with you." The words come out before I've even considered the implications of them. I instantly want to pull them back, having insensitively thrown my request on top of his heavy words, but he instantly lightens up.

"I would love that."

We exchange contacts on our comms. In two days, I've expanded my contacts beyond regular clients and into something more along the lines of friends. Lekka is still just a coworker, but I hope our connection turns into a friendship.

I *need* it to turn into a frienship.

All too soon, he says he has to go. I don't want him to leave so soon. I want to sit here and talk until the sun starts sinking behind the horizon. It has been so long since I've met people who seem to help fill the hole my parents' absence left in me.

With a murmured goodbye, he joins the crowd and vanishes. I stay for a few moments longer. I watch the faces go by, searching for any sort of familiarity. I've worked with enough people to have a grasp of the faces in the Spire. It used to be that once I saw a face, I never forgot it, but that hasn't been the case lately.

In the last year or so, many of my memories have begun to feel strange. It's as if they happened to me, but not quite. Instead, it feels like watching someone else live my life. I wonder if the strain of helping other people see their memories has damaged my own. It's a scary thought, one I don't want to linger on for too long.

I just wish I had someone to talk to about it, someone who understands what it is to take on memories. The only person who could really explain my problem is my mother, but I don't know if I'll ever see her again. She's long gone, another person I will probably begin to forget one day. Especially since she hasn't given me much reason to put effort into remembering her.

I return my dishes to the shop and head home. In learning to listen to myself, I've started building boundaries. I don't stay in public for longer than what feels comfortable. I've found I have a limit for social interaction and it's one I take seriously.

Perhaps the reason this all started is because I never listened to my body. Every ache, every warning was too small to notice on its own, but they built up enough for me to be unable to ignore them any longer.

If I'd listened sooner, maybe I wouldn't

have burnt out in such a severe manner.

◊◊◊

Midnight finds me awake and struggling. The pain of memories came while I was asleep, and now I feel as though I'm drowning. My body shakes and I lay on my side, trying to distract myself with the sight of Argysi.

A shooting star streaks across the sky.

A trail of satellites blink in the distance.

The universe has never felt so small. How does a place with billions, if not trillions, of life-forms manage to make them all feel so out of place? Why couldn't I have been born into a place I was happy in? Why am I suddenly so discontent and weighed down by everything around me?

The first tears come reluctantly. They pave the way for more as the oceans of my mind pour from my eyes, soaking my pillow. I lay there for what feels like an eternity. I just want someone to notice my pain.

Why do I struggle to ask for help?

It's like I've placed an expectation on other people to notice I need help before I can tell them about my pain. I forget that they can't see beneath my skin. I wish we were all a little better at reading each other. Then perhaps understanding would wash away the pain.

When I pass people, I often wonder if they look the same inside as they do outside. What emotions do they carry? Is there blazing anger behind their eyes? Silent confusion? Drowning sorrow?

I'm used to being the outlet through which everyone dumps their emotions, but for once I want to let it loose on someone else. Emotions are like wild animals. They need prey.

Why am I always the prey?

Signed,

one who is tired of running

SEVEN

I tighten the straps of the harness and pull on them, making sure it won't slip off. Lekka watches me in amazement. "I still can't believe you've been coming up here on your own and using the harnesses without getting caught."

I shrug. "I checked to make sure it wasn't against the rules."

"Ever heard of unspoken rules?" She's done with her harness and comes over to double check mine.

"I figure if it's not in writing, it's not serious enough to worry about. Can't blame me for needing a place to think."

"Most of us think in our beds, not hundreds of feet above the ground." She pats my shoulder. "You're all set."

Despite the gentle chastisement, I know

for a fact she feels the same about this place. I've seen how comfortable she is up here, seen the peace that washes over her. She knows as well as I do that thinking inside is not the same; too often it feels as though the thoughts completely fill the room, leaving no space to breathe. I could suffocate in a room of my thoughts. That's how heavy they get.

None of that exists out here. It's an infinite space to hold whatever we let loose. Maybe that's why memories live in the sand. It's a way of loosening their hold on our lives. Only sometimes they get passed on to the wrong people and it leaves more brokenness in its wake.

I don't understand Argysi. It's a strange place.

I help Lekka grab the supplies. She gets the nutrients, which have been refilled during the night. There's a lab on the Spire that makes up a batch every day. I fill our bottles with water. I spent all yesterday dreaming of this moment. I can't wait to let myself fall over the edge. It only took one day of gardening for me to discover my love for it—a much greater love than I ever thought I'd have for an activity.

I feel the cost of it, too. My body is stiff today. The places where the harness sits tight are burning and every time I move my arms, my shoulders groan. I won't let it get to me. I prefer the physical toll to the mental toll. At least I know my body will get used to the harness.

Once we're ready, we balance over the edge. Argysi is silent today, the wind so gentle I hardly feel it.

"Still got the jitters?" Lekka asks.

I shake my head. "I'm ready." I tilt back, my feet securing me to the Spire. Without warning, Lekka throws herself off the side of the Spire. I scream, watching her launch herself out, her body giving itself to the sky. My body freezes and I almost lose my footing. I would've dropped if my rope wasn't taut. Heart racing in my chest, I watch as the ropes slow her descent.

A moment later, it begins pulling her up. She's a dark splotch on the side of the Spire. I'm surprised she didn't knock any gardens down with her reckless behavior. Part of me respects her for the freedom she exudes within her job, but the other part is jealous. I take a breath through the oxygen tube, relishing the cool air that fills my lungs. My legs shake and my heart is still trying to find its rhythm.

"What was that?" I yell. "Give me a warning next time. I almost had a heart attack!"

Her laugh rises, so loud and full. "You should've seen the look on your face."

I bite my tongue, embarrassment on full display. I'm just glad none of the other gardeners are out yet. I wouldn't want them to witness my overreaction. I focus on finishing my climb over the edge. My feet grab the side of the Spire. They feel less steady now that I've seen her fall, and muted fear nudges my mind. She'd spoken of freefalls before and I'd seen people do it yesterday, but watching her jump off the edge was a different feeling altogether.

"Don't do that again. Not without warning me."

She makes her way up beside me, her face more alive than I've ever seen. She grabs onto the small ladder for support. "You got it. One day, I'll get you to jump too."

"How did you not hit anything?" I look down to verify that the gardens are all hanging in their positions.

"I know where the gardens are more than I know my own body. It's all about knowing how far out to jump." She relaxes, the rope holding her in place. Even in the dark, I see warmth creeping across her skin. Even though it's cold, we'll work up a sweat before long.

I look forward to the day I feel as free as Lekka on these ropes. Part of me still worries about them snapping. I don't trust them with my life. Not yet. Not the way I should.

Once we reach the first hanging garden, we work in silence. I don't want to be the one to speak first. As this is Lekka's territory, I leave it to her to decide how much we speak. When she said she was lonely, I think she mostly wanted someone to be with her. She is a loud woman when it suits her, but she can be quiet and contemplative.

"Do you mind if I ask you some questions about yourself?"

I look over at her. Her eyes are resting on me. I know she's looking at some of the things that make me appear different: the sharper turn of my cheeks, the longer ears, the thin hair. Though she's not watching what she's doing, her hands haven't stopped working. Gardening is a deft piece of work—her form of art. She could do it with her eyes closed.

"Sure. I don't mind." I push back against the part of myself that's scared to open up.

"What's it like being half-human and half-spyren?"

I sense some hesitation in the question.

It's not a bad question, or an uncommon question, but it is an uncomfortable one. Something I've learned about humans is how focused they are on identity and their feelings. They place a lot of value in knowing other people's experiences, as well as sharing their own. It's a good thing, I just don't know how to fit my own life into that yet.

Before she returned to them, my mother told me a bit about the spyrens. From what she told me, it was easy to conclude how connected they are to one another. With their feelings flowing in the sand, they're able to know each other on a level humans can't comprehend. Because of that connection, they have no need for the humans' emotional discussions.

"It's frustrating," I admit. "I feel stuck between the Spire and the desert. I want to experience both, but I'm stuck here because I'm spyren enough to feel the memories but not spyren enough to control them."

She nods. "That must be tough. I'm really sorry."

I try not to think about it, but most days it's an all-consuming dread that filters into everything I do. I wish I could learn to keep my pain and uncertainty in the background of my life. It's a pain I'm desperate to leave behind me.

"I think the hardest part is trying to find support. With both my parents gone, I've been making my own way for the past couple years. It's hard."

"Are they dead?"

I shake my head. "My mother left when I was seven. She wanted to go back to the desert and my father couldn't follow her there. He left a couple years ago; said he couldn't live here anymore, too many memories."

There are always too many memories. The echo of my family lingers in every hall. I just can't leave it all behind. I rely on those echoes to remind me of what's real.

"I'm sorry. No one deserves to go through that." She pats the dirt, and we move down to the next row of plants. "So why are you here? What made you choose gardening?"

"I'm trying to take a sabbatical, but it's starting to look more like I'm quitting my job. I don't think I can do it anymore."

"You're a fast learner and you're able to put up with me, so clearly, it's the job and not you. I don't think you'd quit something if it wasn't worth quitting. I won't pretend to know how memory reading works, but I knew of you before you came here. Everyone in the Spire knows of you to some extent."

I shudder. "Do people talk about me?"

She laughs at that, and it takes me by surprise. "Of course, people talk about you. You used to be talked about all the time, back when you were younger. Everyone wanted to know more about the girl who was half human and half spyren. The talk has died down a little, but you're still mentioned. Especially since you took a sabbatical."

I never knew I was part of strangers' daily conversations. The thought of my name on other people's tongues makes me uncomfortable. I have no control over the narrative they spin. Perhaps that was my mother's reason for being detached from the Spire, why she preferred to stay home with me, even though I begged and begged to go out all the time.

She had been hiding me from words she couldn't control.

"Are there people who don't like me?"

"Do you really want to know that?" Lekka's hands have stopped now, and she watches me warily.

I nod, desperate for the truth.

"People here are very accepting, but it can be hard for some of them to accept what they don't understand. There are definitely people who think you're some strange anomaly."

The discourse around my birth is uncomfortable. Some people think I shouldn't exist. "But ... I'm not the only one," I protest.

"You were the first, though."

I was the first, which I hadn't realized until I was older. Any others born over the years have grown up in other Spires. While I was growing up, my mother would always talk about the other half-humans as if their existence was proof that I was acceptable. We'd never approached the topic with the consideration that I'd made other people think about it differently, that I'd paved the way for others like me. Maybe that doesn't make me an end ... maybe it makes me a beginning.

"I bet the same people who think I shouldn't exist are the ones who came to me for their memories," I say bitterly.

She nods, annoyance crossing her face. "The older you get, the more you'll learn that people have a problem with something until it benefits them. It's stupid and hypocritical, but it can't be changed. It's human nature."

Another thing I've learned about human nature is that it's often used to sum up the mistakes of others. When they act out, it's the "human" part of them, they say. I wonder when being human became synonymous with being destructive.

"I don't think human nature is an excuse. It's also human nature to change and grow based on experiences."

"You're right. Of course, you're right."

"And what about you? What do you think of me?" I kick away from the wall and sit in the air. The soft wind plays around my body, a current that rocks me back and forth.

She copies my position and twists to face me. "My father told me I was never to judge anyone without getting to know them first. He said humans are liars and all around awful when they talk about people who aren't in the room. I always judge people based on their actions. Up until a couple days ago, I hadn't known you enough to form an opinion. Now that I know more about you, I can say you're a wonderful, kind person."

I'm unable to keep the smile off my face. "Thank you."

Lekka chuckled. "You know, I almost

didn't offer you the job. I was so scared this would turn out poorly and cause more issues than it was worth. I'm so glad it has gone in the other direction."

"Me too." I'm so glad she gave me this opportunity. I don't know what I would've done in her shoes. "Do you think other people will begin to see who I really am?"

"If they get to know you, of course they will. I don't think there's a mind on the Spire that can't be changed." She reaches out and pats my knee. "Don't think too much about it. If you live your life based on other people's reactions, you'll never truly live."

The black hole in me that's been waiting for some form of love feels a little smaller. I want to reach out and hug her, but it's hard with this much space between us. I'm suddenly aware of the other gardeners starting to work around us.

"Can I tell you something? You have to promise not to laugh."

Laughter is already building in her chest. I can see it in her eyes. "Ask me not to laugh and I'll only laugh harder. Just tell me."

"My therapist told me that in order to improve my life, I need to make friends. I started this hoping I would meet a friend and I think I have."

Her face lights up. "Of course you have! I can never have too many friends. Good friends, that is. I'm glad to be counted among yours."

"You're actually my only friend right now," I say, laughing as I realize how absurd that sounds. Her laughter echoes louder than mine, ringing across the curved surface of the Spire.

◊◊◊

We finish the gardening later than planned. After our first conversation, we couldn't stop talking. The words poured out of us like water from a burst pipe. I feel lighter now than ever before. For the first time, I have someone willing to listen to me. Someone other than my therapist. It's a wonderful feeling.

Since I'm new to all this "friend stuff", I decide to let her take all the first steps. While we're putting away our gear, she asks if I'm interested in joining her for drinks in the evening. I must make a face because she tells me I don't have to drink anything I don't want to; she just appreciates the company.

When I tell her I've never even tried alcohol, she brushes it off and says it's overrated. I like her reactions to the things I tell her. She doesn't give me a hard time for the way I was raised or make fun of the fact that I've truly done so little in my short life. I'm living through the years where I'm supposed to be exploring life, but instead I've been trapped within my own body.

I might try new things now that I have someone to try them with.

We leave with a time to meet, then part ways when the elevator opens on her floor. I lean against the wall, my heart full.

My hands are covered in dirt, and I smell of sweat. As soon as my door is closed behind me, I peel off my sticky clothes and run for the shower. I'm a firm believer in short showers. For my entire life, I've done them as fast as possible, washing my hair, scrubbing my skin, and trying to make myself look presentable in as little time as possible.

Today, however, I take my time. I let the hot water burn the morning off my skin. It's nice to enjoy it without worrying about my schedule.

I wonder if I want to go out and try to find Alix. I have enough time between now and meeting Lekka, I could maybe see if he's painting.

He's the other highlight of my day, but I haven't quite figured out how to balance my social battery properly. I don't want to find him and talk to him, only to be burned out and tired this evening.

I decide not to go by, the day flying past. I want to save all of my energy for tonight. Lekka deserves a fully charged version of myself. Even though I've been staying away from the sand, I'm more perceptive to the emotions of people near me. I take them in without realizing it. It's something I'm trying to work on, I just don't know where to start.

Lekka knocks on my door as the sun begins to touch the horizon. This is my favorite time of day, when the Spire gets enveloped in the most beautiful hue of purple. Every level is steeped in it.

We travel down to floor fifteen. I've been here before in the background and I'm familiar with the atmosphere, yet as the doors open, nervous anticipation floods my body. I feel different stepping out with Lekka at my side. I haven't come to hide behind other people's experiences. I'm here to make my own memories.

"I know you've been here before. Stop acting so nervous," she says, her eyes twinkling with amusement.

"Sorry," I blush, "I've just never been on this floor for this type of thing."

"Well you'd better get used to it. I'm planning on dragging you around with me everywhere I go."

I grin. "I'd like that."

We walk into a small bar. A few people are scattered throughout, though Lekka mentioned we'd be showing up before the majority of the crowd. I follow her as she weaves her way through the tables and claims a booth at the back.

Her name is called out a couple times, people waving at her. She yells things back, totally comfortable with the crowd. I sit in the corner, feeling unsure of myself, as she yells out my name and introduces me to friends. The curiosity builds. My name pulls on knowledge of who I am, and people begin sneaking glances at me. My earlier conversation with Lekka makes me more aware of them.

I fight the desire to sink under the table and never come out.

"Don't worry about it. Everyone here is nice. You might even make some friends," Lekka assures me.

I don't want to doubt her. I want to believe

this will work out for me, even if I'm not sure this setting is going to be my favorite; it's too unpredictable. When I meet with my therapist, she'll be shocked at everything I accomplished in a couple weeks. I've been so busy, I've neglected my journal. I don't need to write my feelings down when I can talk with Lekka. Is this the new normal?

More people pour in. A woman comes over to ask us what drinks we want, and Lekka ends up talking so much that the woman sits down and joins us for a moment. I look around at the other workers. Between taking orders and making drinks, they're taking time to interact with the customers.

"Is this your first time here?" the woman at our table asks. Her hair is dyed bright purple and hangs freely around her shoulders. She tucks some behind an ear as she waits for a response.

"Yeah. I've never ... done this type of thing before."

"Well, Lekka has either done the right thing bringing you here or she has ruined partying for you. I don't know who brings a young person to an old person party. We're boring," she laughs.

"I like this. It's nice." I enjoy watching

the servers as they interact with the people in the room. I know they can't know everyone in the Spire, but they do their best to make sure everyone feels they belong. It's exactly the type of atmosphere I've been longing for.

Before I know it, more people have joined our table. The novelty of a spyren being present wears off as a few drinks trickle out. I choose not to drink, wanting to keep a clear head on this first night, and I'm not the only one taking it easy. Most people are working their way through one or two drinks over the course of the evening.

Lekka is in her element again. She's acting the way she does when she's gardening. Her voice is free and loud as she takes over the crowd with her funny stories. Laughter and cheering fill the room. Two people take it upon themselves to stand on a table beside us and act out Lekka's tales. The servers keep a careful eye on them, laughing with the rest of the room.

Time passes by too quickly. The sunset fades to a dark purple as the sun vanishes and the moon spins into darkness. I nod off as the voices grow quieter. A woman sings. I don't know if she's in the room or if it's a recording. My eyes grow heavier and heavier.

Lekka looks at me and laughs. "You're the

young one here. You shouldn't be falling asleep on us." She starts collecting her things. Other people are leaving too. The sky outside is dark, Oviun rotating slowly, blocking out a swatch of stars.

Lekka guides me home. I'm drained. Though it had been a lot of fun, the effects of being around so many people are starting to sink in. I try to hide my yawns as we get on an elevator and make our way to my apartment. I've only been inside for a moment before I stumble toward my bed and fall fast asleep.

EIGHT

When I was younger, I'd spend hours people-watching, copying their mannerisms, trying to smile how they smiled and laugh how they laughed. It fed my need to feel more human. I fell out of the habit when I started reading memories; I forged a much deeper connection to people then—something far too intimate. That's why I started avoiding them.

Today, I can't stop studying Alix. He sent me a message this morning and invited me to join him. We're making rounds through the market to find more plants for him to paint with. He's constantly experimenting with them, trying to find the best colors. I've enjoyed watching him interact with the sellers. When he talks, he's so open and honest. His smile never fades, and his questions never end. His endless curiosity with the world around him will never cease to amaze me.

He knows most of the people on a first name basis. Each time he introduces me, I smile awkwardly and feel out of place. This is a whole side to his world that I'm seeing for the first time. He pulls a small cart behind him, which has been rapidly filling over the course of the morning. Some booths have given us entire bins full of plants, while others have given us little bags to sample.

He's talking to a woman named Fyeri. She's one of the last sellers. She runs a drying rack and sells all sorts of dried plants and dehydrated foods. She shows us how to lay the plants out on heat racks to remove the moisture from them. Beside her, a dehydrator hums.

I don't speak. I want to watch and be helpful, but not get in the way. I've been learning a lot about his art. Enough to know that it's very personal to him. He treats it with intense care, as if it's the very purpose of his existence. He asks me for my opinions a lot. I don't think I know enough to have well-formed advice, but I appreciate that he cares about what I think.

The variety of plants I've seen today is fascinating. Some of them are grown on Argysi, but the majority of them are imported. How do they know what plants to order?

"I actually ordered something special for you last time," Fyeri says excitedly. She reaches into a compartment under her stand and pulls out some tubs. "I remembered you mentioning your struggle to find a good yellow. Yellow is a weaker color, and I knew you'd need something strong." She opens a tub and hands it to Alix.

I peek in. A long vine sits coiled on the bottom. Hanging from it are several large, yellow flowers.

Alix grins. "Where did you get these?"

"I can't reveal my secrets, but I've been told they make a strong dye. I'm not sure if they'll be any good for painting. Try them out, free of charge." She reaches in and lifts one of the flowers. With a gentle press of the petals, yellow fluid runs down her fingers. "I assume you'll want to try them fresh first. If you want any dried, just come back. I want to know how they work."

"Of course," Alix promises. He adds the tub to the cart.

We continue on, weaving our way across the floor until we've talked to everyone he's interested in. Time has marched on steadily. We started early when the floor was mostly empty. It's now bursting with energy.

"Do you want to get lunch?" Alix asks.

"Yes. I'm dying of hunger," I laugh. My stomach has been quietly growling for the past hour. A beast is about to be awoken inside me if I don't eat something.

"Sorry. I didn't realize it would take so long."

"It seems everyone wants to talk to you."

He smiles. "You know, the first time I came through here, it only took a couple minutes. I got what I wanted and left. No one really cared. Now it seems everyone has heard of what I'm doing and they're all curious."

Over the past couple days, his table has been crowded by curious bystanders. Word of his edible paint and brilliant portraits have spread through the Spire. While it means I enjoy less of his company, I'm so proud of his success.

We step into the elevator and ride it to a floor of his choosing. He clearly has a place in mind to eat and since I'm not a picky eater, I don't mind him choosing. When the doors open, we're greeted by the smell of food and the vast selection of restaurants and food stalls. The businesses line the outer walls of the Spire, leaving the center space full of tables and chairs. Most diners have finished their meals, leaving many of the tables empty. My stomach growls loudly this time and Alix looks at me with a grin.

We claim a table, stack the supplies on it, and I settle down. He asks me what I'd like before running off to find it, face tight with concentration, glasses askew. Even though he apologized for taking so long in the market, I wouldn't have dreamed of rushing him. I treasure every slow moment I can spend getting to know him more and learning everything he has to offer through his words. I loved seeing people treat him the way he deserves to be treated and the same way he treats them.

Picking up the food doesn't take long and only a few minutes later, he comes back, catching me watching him. "What?" He smiles, unsure.

"Nothing," I say, reaching for the food.

He pauses, his eyes searching mine, then shrugs it off and sits down. We eat in a calm sort of silence.

◊◊◊

"Tell me about your life before Argysi." I look over at Alix. The late afternoon light frames his face perfectly. We're sitting on a bench facing the glass. After we ate, he brought the plants up to his home and now we're relaxing before the evening takes over. He's planning to paint, while I'm planning to sit in my room and add to my journal.

His face shadows for a moment. "There really isn't much to say," he offers weakly.

"Sorry, I shouldn't have brought it up."

"No, it's fine. You should know. I just don't like to think about it much, it's a lot of hard memories."

I nod and try to understand. I have lots of experience with hard memories, but only a few of them are my own.

"Okay, then don't focus on that yet. Is this the first Spire you came to?"

"Nope. I started in the Hub." He leans back, his eyes tilting toward the ceiling. "Have you ever been there?"

"Nope." I've never traveled to another Spire. The Hub is the largest Spire on Argysi and it's where the transports land when bringing in tourists or new citizens. Most of the people coming in from other planets choose to arrive at the Hub. Many of them never leave, content with the life there. "Why'd you leave?"

"I didn't for a while. It took me a few months to realize the Hub wasn't what I wanted. It's not bad, but it's so similar to everywhere else. All the tourists and newcomers bring in the sort of culture I came here to avoid. Trust me when I say this Spire is much better. The people here are gentle, and everything moves at a quieter pace."

I hum in agreement. I want him to speak when he's ready, without me pushing the words out of him. I'm scared that if I push him, it will ruin the ties between us. I just want to know how I can help him. When he paints, I catch glimpses of a hollow part of himself, and I know he has a lot happening inside his head.

"I come from a planet called Detrius. Ever heard of it?"

I shake my head. I don't know much about the universe beyond the moon, and since I never plan to leave, it feels like useless information.

"It's an industrial planet. The lowest of the low. I don't think anyone there is happy. The planet is dying beneath the industries, yet no one's going to stop draining it. They'll just keep taking and taking until there's nothing else for it to give."

"What types of industries?"

"A little bit of everything. They drill for oil, they mine for minerals. I don't think there's a place on that planet that's unscathed. It's all work sites and crowded cities." He gestures at the desert in front of us. It's so vast and empty, we can't even see the next closest Spires. "There's no space like this. It's claustrophobic."

I shudder. "What did you do?"

"Same as everyone else. I survived. I don't like to think about my job. While working, it was best for me to empty my mind, so I didn't bring any of that trauma home. Not that it mattered. My dad died when I was young, and he was the one who really cared for me and my sister. My mom married again, and life went to hell. It was constantly me against them." He pauses and swallows, the silence eating away at us for the next couple minutes.

I want to offer my hand to him, to show him I care and am here to listen. Instead, I curl it in my lap and wait for him to start again.

"I was never supposed to leave. I planned to stick around for my sister's sake. She couldn't survive on her own, not in the type of house we grew up in. But she died and it broke something in me. I did things I'm not proud of and I got out of there. I think if I hadn't, I would've died too.

There's no living on that planet. Not for someone like me." A tear runs down his face. He wipes it away, but another appears soon after, following the trail of the first.

"I'm sorry." I reach out.

He shifts, then stands. "I have a painting session I need to prepare for. Thank you for keeping me company today, August. It was a lot of fun. And thank you for ... everything else."

I nod. "Of course. Message me if you need anything."

He says he will and walks off, leaving me alone beneath the weight of his past.

◊◊◊

I spend an hour before bed watching the stars, imagining everything that's spread out between them. There are so many lives in the universe, so many beings filled with joy and pain. It seems the two emotions cannot exist on their own. They are counterparts. After talking with Alix, I've grown more aware of the bubble around Argysi. It's a peaceful moon and it cares for those who live on it.

Alix messages me to thank me for listening. I read the message and cradle my comm to my chest. I imagine him in his own home, alone in the darkness, a gnawing sadness inside him. I've lived a sheltered life. In all my frustrations, I've forgotten what it means to live in an unforgiving universe.

There is so much I want to write I could fill pages and pages of everything I've felt over the past couple days, but it would all come down to one thing. Freedom.

There is beauty in holding the future in my hands.

There is peace in waking up with hope.

I feel like I've fallen into the spot that life was waiting for me to find.

Everyone understands what it's like to be lonely. I think that's why some people, like Alix, try so hard to help everyone feel loved. But this sense of belonging is such a new and strange thing. If only I'd known there were places I could go where people would accept me.

I'm beginning to understand the cost of freedom. I've heard things I would've never imagined and seen glimpses of lives that seem impossible to live.

I'm learning it's a fickle thing, this balance of happiness and reality.

Signed,

one who is beginning to understand

NINE

Time moves faster now that I'm able to find joy in living. The days are no longer stretched out. I'm not dragging my feet through the dregs of life. Days are ending sooner than I want. It feels like the moon is spinning faster, the sun vanishing quicker.

The weeks speed by.

My days have fallen into a routine I love. I garden, I explore the Spire, I hang out with Lekka at various places, and I continue building a friendship with Alix. A wall has been torn down between us ever since he told me about his past.

Before I know it, I wake up greeted with a reminder of my next therapy session. I roll over, tapping the notification to remove it from my comm. I've been so busy I forgot about therapy. Now that it's just a couple hours away, I wonder how I'm supposed to talk about the massive change that's happened in my life.

I've gotten better at speaking my thoughts and I no longer rely on my journal. I don't think my journal can encapsulate the way I feel at this moment. The joy filling every crevice in my soul is something a pen could not put to paper.

I set about getting myself ready, pulling on clothes and making myself breakfast. I cut up three peryns, small fruit with sweet, pink flesh, and mix them into a bowl with an assortment of nuts. I eat by the window, letting the peace of Argysi wash over me. When the time comes, I tuck my journal under my arm and leave the comfort of my apartment.

◊◊◊

Cora is surprised when I don't hand her the journal right away. Instead, I keep it pressed between my hands, nervous energy running through my fingers.

"Good morning, August," she greets me, a wide smile filling her face. She looks expectantly at the journal.

"Good morning."

"How are you doing?"

A loaded question: one that normally prompts me to hand over the journal. Today, I open my mouth and let an abbreviated account of the last couple weeks pour out. Cora sits back, eyes wide, and listens while I talk about the gardens, my relationship with Lekka, the evenings I've spent out, Alix, his paintings, and the way I'm feeling better about myself than I ever have before.

Once I start, I can't stop. Cora doesn't try to interject or slow me down. She just soaks it in, at points closing her eyes, resting between the current of my words.

In spite of the many sessions I've had, I've never felt this *listened* to. As I speak, I fully grasp the weight of my growth. I've dug myself a place to live in, and now I'm ready to begin blooming.

When I finally reach the end, a full minute of silence stretches between us.

"I'm so proud of you," Cora says, glowing. "I've been worried about you the last few weeks. I even thought about trying to book our appointment earlier. Instead, you went out there and grabbed the world with both your hands. You've taken control of what's rightfully yours."

I like that phrase. I've *grabbed the world with both my hands.* What a satisfying thing to say.

"I thought it would be much harder, but now that I'm here, I don't know why I wasn't here sooner. I feel like I've sacrificed so many years for nothing. I could've been happy the entire time."

"But you reached that conclusion much earlier than some people. I've spoken to people at the end of their life who are just beginning to realize how much freedom they could've had if they'd just went for it. There is nothing quite as sad as someone realizing their entire life could've been fuller."

We sit in that sentence for a moment. I can't believe how happy I am right now. It's almost concerning, the amount of joy building up within me. It's like a disease. Once it starts, it just keeps multiplying, spreading further into everything I say and do. But I like that.

I want people to look at me and *see* the happiness sitting on my shoulders. I want them to wish they had my life, just as I used to wish I had theirs.

"So, is this it? You're going to quit reading memories and move into gardening full-time?"

"I think so, yeah. I haven't announced anything, but I can't imagine going back to my previous job." Actually, I'd rather die than go back. If I placed myself in that cage again, knowing the freedom that lies beyond, I think it would kill me.

"For the record, I think you need to quit. You are doing so much better now," Cora says.

"I just ... worry. Not about quitting, but about this new job catching up to me."

"You will never find a place in life where you are constantly happy. There will always be hard days. It's knowing you can find happiness no matter where you are that matters."

I know I have to come to terms with that. Gardening will sometimes feel like a chore, and I won't be excited every morning; I've already woken up wanting a couple more hours of sleep. But after I wake up and force myself to get ready, that desire gives way to excitement for the hours of work ahead of me. Those negative moments are outweighed by the positive, and that's what matters.

At the end of the session, Cora gives me a hug. She holds me tight, as if scared I'll vanish between her fingers, and she tells me she's proud of me. I battle tears when I leave her office.

◊◊◊

I sit on a bench and take a minute to watch as the morning shifts to afternoon. I don't want to face my empty apartment right now, but I do have private business to take care of. I open my laptop and click onto my website. I haven't touched it in the weeks I've been gone. Though I'd silenced the notifications, queries hadn't ceased flooding in. Many of them are asking when I'm coming back, others are offering to trade their services if I'll help them, all of them ignore that I'm on a sabbatical.

Once, I took pride in my website. It was a public display of what I believed mattered. I used it to build my clients, to prove my worth. Now, it all seems pointless. I don't need to prove myself to anyone. My worth was never in reading memories, it was simply in existing. And that was enough.

A large list of clients I'd spent the last five years curating stares back at me. I scroll through the names, trying not to think how not a single one of them had asked me how I was doing, or why I was even taking a sabbatical. The memories of giving myself over and over to these people hits me like a glass wall. My stomach tightens.

Without any more hesitation, I shut down my website. It takes only minutes to go through the motions, ignore all the warnings, and completely wipe it from the Spire's database. I tense, waiting for a moment of regret, for those pesky second thoughts to get to me.

But they never come.

TEN

The first time I ask Alix to my home, he freezes, and I immediately regret it. He apologizes, saying he doesn't feel ready to come to my home yet. I understand. While we've spent several afternoons together, that doesn't compare to the sacredness of home. Entering someone else's space is one of the biggest steps in a friendship.

He accepts the second time after I ask him to teach me to paint. I spend two hours trying to clean and organize, even though I don't own a lot. My bedroom is mostly empty, aside from the bed, a place for my clothes, and the painting on my wall. The rest of my apartment is occupied by a couch and the kitchen. A few things left by my parents are the only sparse decor I have. After they left, I cleared out their room and moved my own belongings into it, turning my old bedroom into an extension of the living space. I leave their small personal touches alone, hoping that maybe one day they'll come back and find a home that has been waiting for them.

I know Alix won't judge my living space. He's much too polite. Still, I stress needlessly because I don't know how else to cope with him coming over.

I survey the supplies I've strewn across the table: several canvases and a couple mugs. He's bringing the paint. I'm excited to see what colors and flavors we get.

In the days I've watched him, I've never seen the exact same shade. He says that's part of the beauty of art; no art is ever identical because no artist ever sees things the same way twice. Each color and line is purposely used to give the viewer insight into the artist's vision.

A knock on the door startles me. I run my hands down the front of my shirt, nerves shooting through me, and swing the door open.

He comes in, smiling as nervously as I feel, trying to get comfortable and oriented inside a space that doesn't belong to him. I see him trying to settle, his body tight as he lays the mixtures across the table.

"Do you have a kettle?" he asks.

"Yeah." I lead him into the place where

I live. Hopefully he can begin to feel at home here. I need new memories to chase out the same haunting emptiness that greets me morning and night.

We boil water and he lets me help with the mixtures. I've never helped make the paint before, and it's exciting to be part of the process. Each bag has dried plants. Some are crushed, others are cut into pieces. During his public painting sessions, I hover in the crowd and try not to take his attention away from everyone else.

"How did you start doing this?" Dried flowers fall out as I dump one of the bags into a mug.

He shrugs. "I did something similar when I was younger. It was my escape. Since coming here, I've had more time to experiment. I just go with whatever happens." He picks up the kettle and fills the mugs.

The one in front of me changes colors the quickest. It starts as a light color, then darkens rapidly. The amount of purple a single dried flower held shocks me. It's like watching a sunset on Argysi.

Alix sets a strainer on top of another mug and pours the purple water into it, leaving the sprigs behind. "I didn't expect them to be that strong. I'll have to use less next time." He swishes the paint around, marveling at the strong color.

"I want to use that," I say, reaching for it. I've got an idea of what I want to paint. I've never painted before and I don't know how to take the idea in my head and make it come to life. I'm going to start by painting what I see. As I look at Argysi, I'm filled with the need to put that view down on a canvas.

"Here, start with a background." He hands me a larger paintbrush. "What do you want to paint?"

"The moon." I look over my canvas, trying to envision Argysi in the colors before me.

"Then you'll also want this." He pushes a mug over that holds a pink color. "You're very lucky. The colors are exactly what you need."

I can't help but grin. Everything feels perfect today. The sun is on the other side of the Spire, allowing me to observe the moon through my windows without a glare. I'm not sure where to start. How does one take a couple colors and turn it into something they love?

I watch Alix's process. He prefers to paint faces. Not just portraits of people he's seen, but faces of creatures I'm not sure even exist. He always works with small lines first, setting up an idea to fill in later. It's such a different process from what I feel is necessary. The moon is not something to be sketched in little lines. It needs strong, confident strokes.

The brush soaks up the pink mixture so easily. I pull it out, dripping it across the canvas. I want this painting to look raw. Argysi is an imperfect moon, covered in spots and craters and oceans of sand. As the spots soak into the canvas, I start wiping the brush lightly across the entire canvas. The light pink hue is perfect to set up the background. It fuses with the spots, leaving darker imprints across it.

Each stroke feels like a piece of the breeze. With my hand, I have begun to capture the wildness of the moon. I am scattering the sand with my fingers, controlling the weather with the flick of my wrist.

I look for a smaller brush and begin working with the dark purple. I use it around the craters, coloring them like bruises. The dark bleeds into the light and begins seeping into the rest of the painting. I try to guide the lines. They reach like fingers, stretching across until I feel this is no longer my painting. This is *our* painting—mine and the colored water that has a mind of its own.

A couple hours pass before I feel finished. I've been mixing and layering, working on building up an accurate image of the chaos and peace that I feel sits beyond the Spire. In that time, I've entered my own space. I don't feel tethered to my body. It's like I'm part of Argysi, feeling the very soul of the moon, and it's the most beautiful thing I've ever experienced.

If this is how Alix feels when he paints people, I wonder what he felt when he painted me. I wonder if he knows more about me than I realize. I don't know what my soul feels like. The very inner core of myself is not something I'd consider myself well acquainted with.

It's something I tend to avoid.

When I set the brushes down, the world comes flying back all at once. I'm jolted to reality: me within these walls, paint on my hands, and Alix looking at me curiously. His dark hair falls over his eyes and he pushes it away with the back of his hand.

"Are you okay?"

I nod. "I'm sorry. I kind of zoned out."

"Don't apologize. Art has to be made in whatever setting feels right for the artist. Can I look?"

I know he can see my painting from where he sits, but his eyes don't look down. He's been giving me privacy and letting me paint without scrutinizing. I look down at it fondly. For someone who has never painted, I feel very proud of it. The colors are perfect, the abstract patterns so obviously echoing the landscape of Argysi.

I slide the painting over to him. Some of the water is still wet and it shifts a little. He takes it from me, his fingers holding the edges gently, careful not to mix anything up. As his eyes move across it, I feel uncomfortably seen. I don't know how he paints with an audience. I want this to go somewhere for me to enjoy on my own. It's not something I could show off.

"This is amazing," he gushes. "You tricked me by telling me you needed a lesson."

I laugh. "I've never painted before. I didn't lie about that."

"Well, for someone who's never painted before, you did an amazing job. This is perfect." He carries the painting over to the glass wall. I follow, a little hesitant to closely compare the painting to its muse.

We stand there in comfortable silence, surveying the landscape for a long time. He hands me my painting and puts an arm around my shoulder. I lean into him, breaking some barrier we were hiding behind, and think about what this means. I feel his smile before I look over and see it.

How nice it is to be two happy people on a purple moon.

I wouldn't trade this moment for anything in the world.

Do good things always end?

I keep thinking I'm in a dream. I pinch myself a couple times a day, positive that all this goodness has been a figment of my imagination. It might be a bad response to everything, but I can't help it. Every good thing in my past has ended, and I'm not sure how to appreciate things for what they are. I always have to look ahead and imagine their downfall.

I don't think I would survive if all this came to an end.

I could never go back to my old life after tasting all this new one has to offer.

I'm scared.

Signed,

one who can't accept the present without knowing the future

ELEVEN

While gardening, Lekka asks if I want to do something with her tonight. Over the past few weeks, she's taken me to all sorts of places, introducing me to a number of people in the Spire. It has been a great experience, but I need something more casual today.

I lean away from the wall and wipe sweat from my forehead. "How would you feel about dinner at my place?"

"I would love that."

I don't know where my invitation came from. If she's going to have dinner with me, I'm going to have to prepare food. I have faint memories of helping my parents make food, but I didn't do much aside from handing them ingredients, and when my mom left, my dad stopped cooking altogether. After that, we got our meals from various bakers. Since his departure, I've mostly done the same.

I used to only like eating food made by other, more talented people. But one thing I've been learning is that I'm capable of developing my own talents if I'm willing to put in the time and energy.

Lekka drifts away. She's heading to the lower gardens.

"Do you mind if I invite another one of my friends? I'd love for you to meet them."

Lekka looks up, her hands on her hips. "Is that even a question? Of course, I want to meet them."

Alix has been over to my place a couple times, and I've grown more comfortable around him and with a paintbrush. My bedroom wall is starting to fill with color. He keeps saying I should paint some things and bring them to the art floor to offer to others, but it's something I need to keep to myself right now.

Anxiety washes over me like a cold breeze. I don't know if Alix is free tonight. I don't even know if he and Lekka will get along. I might not be able to make good food. Tonight could be a failure.

I sink my hands into the dirt, squishing the

nutrients into it. I need to stop thinking for the rest of my shift.

◊◊◊

I send an invite to Alix after my shower. He tells me he'd love to come, then asks if I need help making food. Either he wants to spend more time with me or thinks I'm an awful cook—I'm hoping it's the former. I ask him to meet me on the seventh floor.

I open the highest cupboard above the stove and look at the stack of dusty cookbooks on the top shelf. My father packed them away shortly after she left in an attempt to hide the painful reminders of the time they'd spent cooking together. I haven't looked at them since.

Though I usually prefer whatever is easiest to make or pick up, I decide to make something special tonight. After going through the trouble of inviting friends over and cleaning for them, I should put the same effort into the food.

Even if it turns into a disaster.

Climbing onto the counter, I carefully draw the stack from the shelf. The books are separated between main courses and desserts. I slip out the ones I want and leave the others to their sad disuse.

Flipping through the books, I'm mesmerized by all the colorful pictures of various foods. I want my table to look like this tonight. I mark down ingredients for the specific dishes I want to make and fold the page corners so I can find the recipes later.

Floor seven is packed with food dispensaries and grocery shops full of all sorts of products, both grown and imported. I wait by the elevator until Alix comes out. He's wearing clothes spotted with the watery paint and smells like his art.

"Did I disrupt a painting session?" I reach out and wipe a blue spot from his cheek.

"Nope. An art session was disrupting my time with you." He takes the basket from my hands and offers his other hand to me. I take it, warmth spreading through my body.

"I'm going to be honest. I'm not the greatest cook. I invited Lekka over, and now I have to impress her with something."

"I don't think she expects to be impressed. Just make something simple. Something from the heart. That will be enough." He scans my list, muttering the items under his breath. "I think this is perfect. We can do lots with this."

We head to the first booth and take sparingly, only filling the basket with what we need. Since becoming a gardener, I've become more conscious of the effort it takes to keep the Spire running. I try to take less and give more. It's a mentality I should've always had, but in my emotionally drained state, I never thought much of it.

At each shop, the items we take are scanned to remove them from inventory. It's obvious some of the sellers know who I am. I catch eyes following my movements. I recognize some of the faces I've worked with, and I subtly try to avoid them. I'm expecting someone to bring up the removal of my site at some point, and the thought of having to explain my new life terrifies me.

I grab some tubercles from the next table. They're raw, which means I'll need to mash them if I want to turn them into a crust.

Alix leaves me for a moment, then comes back with a bag of something else. "I hope you don't mind if I improvise on your menu a little," he says, his eyes sparkling.

"Of course not." I'm relieved he's taking this seriously. Without the responsibility of the whole dinner on me, I'm able to find more excitement for tonight.

Life is so much easier with the help of others. I don't know how I did it on my own for so long. Finding the courage to open up and let others into my life is one of the best things I've done.

It only takes us half an hour to find everything we want. The basket is quite full. I just hope we use everything. Alix seems quite confident in our ability to make a fun spread.

When we get back to my home, he instantly takes over the kitchen. I love how comfortable he's become in my kitchen. He knows where everything is, having used much of it for our painting. It feels nice having someone else be familiar with my home. My existence feels more ... present now that I matter to someone beyond myself.

I wash the produce while he grabs bowls and pans and other things I forgot I even owned. I have to laugh as I watch him. I'd be absolutely lost without him.

He looks at the tools he collected. "You have a really good kitchen, you know."

"I didn't know, but I'm glad. I wouldn't know how to stock it on my own."

We fall into a rhythm. I flip back through the cookbooks and show him what I want to make. As I read off the instructions, he shows me how to carry them out. The beginning stages are not very fun. He ends up having to mash the tubercles for me because they're hard and stubborn, the thick skin refusing to split. One of them flies out of the bowl and almost hits me in the face. Alix stops mashing, his eyes wide with concern, and I burst into laughter.

"I didn't realize the tubercles would be so hard to cook with." I reach over the counter and pick up the offending vegetable. All his mashing efforts have barely done anything.

"It has occurred to me that we're probably supposed to boil them before mashing them," Alix says sheepishly.

I pause, brandishing the tubercle like a weapon. "That ... does sound like it would help." We laugh again.

While he fills a pot with water, I slice up the vegetables. We're trying to make a casserole. It should be easy, but neither of us have made one before. The crust is mostly made of mashed tubercles and the inside is whatever vegetables we want. I fry them while the water comes to a boil.

Before long, the kitchen smells amazing. The pan simmers on the stove. Alix is able to mash the tubercles and mix them with other ingredients to make dough. I watch as he slices up little pieces of plants and rolls them into the disk of dough.

"What's that for?" I ask. He slides the dough over for me to knead.

"I'm hoping the herbs add extra flavor to the dough." He speaks while running over to the stove to stop the vegetables from growing too dark.

While we work, we fill the kitchen with endless conversation. I haven't addressed the things he told me about his past, but he has started inserting more memories into our conversations. I find him telling me stories that he sometimes pauses halfway through, as if surprised he's speaking, then continues with a smile. While his life before Argysi was hard, he has a lot of positive memories.

"Would you choose this moon over the entirety of the universe?" I ask, holding my breath.

"I would," he says without hesitation. "What you have here is something so incredibly special. You're surrounded by a caring community of people, and you have the space to develop your gifts and grow as a person. I'm not joking when I say this moon is one-of-a-kind. You're very fortunate to have been born here."

I love hearing someone speak so kindly of my home. I could sink into his words forever. When he speaks, his words carry such light. It's no surprise he's an artist. To him, the world is a place of shapes and colors.

I've started learning to see the world through his eyes, and now I feel I can spot the beauty in everything. While learning to regulate myself and function in the Spire, I've also taken the time to appreciate the tower and everyone in it.

The afternoon passes quickly. Neither of us ate lunch and we taste test as we go to keep ourselves from getting hangry. As the time nears for Lekka to arrive, I can't help but think about all the ways Lekka and Alix are different. They both fill separate needs in my life. Lekka has taught me a lot about being confident and kind. She takes the world in stride, never stressing about what hasn't happened yet. Alix is soft and quiet, letting the world wash over him. He treasures every experience and has taught me to slow down and enjoy the things around me.

I want to be like both of them.

I want them to get along.

I look over at Alix. He's peeking into the oven, poking at the crust to make sure it's fully cooked but not burnt. He blinks as steam fills the air around him, completely fogging up his glasses, then looks up at me and laughs.

"I think we're ready," he says.

I don't know why I'm so worried. Both of my friends are easy going and likeable. It seems impossible for them to *not* like each other. I help him take the food out of the oven. The main course is the casserole. While waiting for it to cook, we made some small side dishes. There's a salad covered in creamy dressing, and vegetable wedges fried in sweet oil. My mouth waters just looking at it all.

"We did it." I give Alix a hug, unable to fully express my gratitude for his help. "Thank you so much."

He tightens his hold and smiles, keeping me close for a moment longer. "You're welcome."

◊◊◊

Lekka shows up with her own little dish of food. I usher her into the home, aware of Alix standing in the kitchen. He's covering the food on the stove with lids to keep it from cooling.

Lekka hands me the glass dish. "I know you said you were making the food, but I felt bad showing up empty handed. I brought a dessert."

I look inside. Small rolls sit in jelly. The steam rising from them is filled with an intoxicating smell. I breathe it in and sigh. "This smells *amazing*."

Alix leaves the stove and comes over to introduce himself. They start chatting and I begin organizing the dishes on the table. I've never had two people over at a time. My home suddenly feels much smaller, but I find it comforting. As a child, my parents were the two constants in my life. They filled this home with their small lives.

They're laughing and the knot of tension in me loosens a little. All the anxiety is in my head; I need to get out of my head and start enjoying the evening for what it is. I let their conversation flow around me. It feels nice to be the cause for people meeting. Opening my home to people who were once strangers but now are friends is a beautiful thing.

When we sit down to eat, the food is even better than I expected. The tastings we had earlier don't even compare to the experience of having a full plate. We eat until we're full, then enjoy a plate of desserts. Lekka has a knack for whipping together food, but she says if we ever want anything from her that's not sweet, she won't be able to do it. Her hands only make sugary food.

The sun sets behind us, and I bask in the last of its warmth. The heat feels thin through the thick glass. It's nowhere near as hot as working outside. Full of food, bursting with contentment, and now resting in the warmth, I tip my chair back a little and grin as I close my eyes.

"Someone looks very happy," Lekka comments. She's working her way through a second roll. Alix has his plate pushed back so he's not tempted to eat more.

"I don't think today could've been more perfect."

"If you two want to keep making suppers this delicious, I won't say no to an invite," Lekka laughs.

"It will definitely happen again," Alix promises. I glow at their words. I'm so glad they want to do this again.

"Alix told me you've been painting together. I didn't know you were an artist, August." Lekka looks around, as if trying to find the pictures. "I would love to see your work. He said you have a portrait that he painted of you."

"They're in my room." I slide out of my chair and leave the kitchen, entering the darker places in my home. They feel hollow without the light and laughter. I look at the paintings on my bedroom wall. Alix's portrait is still my favorite. I've painted several more landscapes since the first one, all of them different versions of Argysi. It seems to be the only thing I know how to paint. Alix says it's my ultimate muse.

I pull them off the wall, stacking them in my hands. I keep the portrait at the bottom. I've enjoyed treasuring these as my own, not feeling the need to share them with anyone else. But today it feels right to share them. I've opened my home, and now I'm opening my heart.

Lekka and Alix wait at the counter. I set down the canvases and Alix helps me lay them out. Lekka looks them over, pausing over each one to really take it in. She praises my landscapes. No one but me and Alix have seen them, so I'm glad she likes them. While painting, I've become intimately familiar with the pockmarked surface of Argysi. Putting it on a canvas feels like a fulfilling purpose.

She picks up the portrait, holding it up to compare to my face. "You're really good." She turns to Alix, grinning.

"Thank you." Alix's face floods with relief.

"Do you think you could paint me sometime? I would love one of these on my wall."

"I would love to paint you."

"Is painting all you do?"

He shakes his head. "I work in the water plant when I'm needed. If a filter needs cleaning, I'm your guy." He laughs.

We look over the paintings for a few more minutes before retreating to the couch, leaving the kitchen a mess. The world outside has grown dark. I like how purple can become so dim, it almost looks black. Argysi has many faces, but its night face is the most intimidating of them all.

We've been talking for a while when my comm beeps, alerting me of an incoming message. I lift my wrist and check it. It's a notice saying I have a visitor ... from the lower entrance of the Spire.

"Uh, guys?" I interrupt their conversation. "My comm says I have a visitor. Someone who came through the lower entrance of the Spire."

"That's strange." Alix looks out the window. "Visitors don't usually come through the lower entrance."

He's right. Most people arrive on the transports, and those land on the roof. Aside from the clients I took out to read memories, the only other people that come through the lower entrances are spyren. Though welcoming to the humans living on their moon, the spyren aren't known for visiting the Spires. Our doors are always open to them, but they prefer to live in constant contact with the sands of Argysi.

My blood runs cold. I only know two people who would visit me. My father, who hasn't bothered to contact me since he left, and my mother. Between the two of them, only my mother could arrive without a transport.

I don't want to believe it, but it's the only possibility that makes sense. But why now? After all this time, she can't make me believe she truly cares about me. I don't have a space in my life waiting to be filled by her.

"You look like you've seen a ghost. Are you okay?" Lekka puts a hand on my shoulder.

"I think it's my mother."

Lekka and Alix exchange looks. I've mentioned enough of my parents for them to know what this means.

"Do you want to see her?" Alix asks.

Up until this moment, I haven't even considered that I have a choice. I don't *have* to go down to meet her. But I can't just leave her alone ... even though she left me. "I don't know. I suppose I'm curious." I sink my face into my hands. This is too much to process. "I don't even know if it's her. I'm just speculating. It could be anyone."

I get up from the couch and look at the kitchen. It's still a mess from dinner and I can't meet my mother for the first time in years only to bring her back to a messy house and two friends. I look around, desperation filling me.

"Go meet her. We'll clean up and leave before you get back. We can continue this another night." Alix is already leaving the couch. Lekka follows him to the kitchen.

"Do you mind?"

"No! Go." He's stacking up the dishes and Lekka is hurrying to put away the leftover food. I back out of the house, watching as they scurry. If I could freeze time with these two, I would. It feels like I've just started making my own way in the world.

Why do ghosts of the past have to show up at the worst times?

TWELVE

She is not the mother I remember.

When I step into the bay, she is standing on the other side, looking out the narrow window on the large doors. Her fingers press against the glass. She seems reluctant to leave the desert behind. Beside her, a small screen glows. It's the message log that allows visitors to find any of the people living in the Spire.

I remember her as a quiet woman. She kept to herself, almost fading away behind the walls of the Spire. I remember her skin being the same pale shade as mine—a blue so light it was almost white. Now she seems larger with her presence. Her skin has grown darker, fuller, filling out her body.

In this way, I know I have lost the mother I remember.

I clear my throat. She turns with a smile,

taking me in all at once. "How you have grown," she says, coming in for a hug.

I open my arms reluctantly. Pulling her in is accepting the weight again. Up close, I smell the desert on her. Stray pieces of sand are caught in her hair. If she was anyone else, I would worry about the memories trapped in them. Since it's her, I know she has already drained them dry.

I stand taller than her. I remember the size difference between her and my father; they had fit together so well, her head just coming up to his chest. With us, it's awkward.

She looks up. "How are you doing?"

"I ... am fine." I settle on an easy word.

Disappointment dulls her eyes. "Just fine? That's all I get after years of not seeing you? I want to know more."

"I just—" I'm exasperated, but I don't know how to say it without tearing my heart in two, "don't understand why you're here. Why come back? Why now?"

"Surely you don't hold resentment for something that happened so long ago?"

I step away from her. "Resentment? You tore my life apart when you left. You tore dad's life apart. You were supposed to be here with me. Instead, I grew up with a shell of a man who just wanted the woman he fell in love with."

Tears glisten in her eyes. "Don't you understand? I couldn't be that for him. Living in here was killing me. I had to leave, whether he understood it or not."

"But you never explained it to *me*. You just vanished one day and never came back. You couldn't even visit?" I'm not taking any of her excuses. "You can't have a child and decide not to take part in raising them. I *needed* you." My voice cracks. Tears threaten to spill over, and I wipe at them angrily. I don't want to cry in front of her.

She opens her arms again, asking for another chance, but I turn and walk out of the room. It's too much.

She follows me. I hear her bare feet on the cold floor, smell the sweat of the sun on her skin, and I know then that she could never thrive in this world. I might not be able to forgive her yet, but I understand that she had to leave, just as I had to leave sand reading. It hurts, yet it's scarily relatable.

It's easy to understand, harder to forgive.

"Listen,—I turn, facing her again—"you

can come up and stay with me and we can figure something out, but it's going to take time for me to feel comfortable around you."

"I can leave," she offers.

"No … that doesn't feel right. You came. The least I can do is take you in for the night."

My words deflate her. I don't know what she expected. An excited daughter willing to pick up where we left off? I can't do that. Not for my sake. It goes against everything I feel in my soul. Offering her a place for the night, without extending it further, gives me enough time to think about what to do.

I don't rush her up to my home. I want to give Lekka and Alix time to get out. The last thing I need is an audience for our show.

The entire trip up feels like an awkward dance that neither of us know the steps to. She stands in the corner of the elevator, her eyes never leaving me, and I shift beneath her gaze like an animal caught in a trap.

"I didn't realize he'd left you," she whispers.

We're almost at my floor.

I feel old wounds opening. It's not fair that

I've spent so long stitching them closed, only for her to come in and undo all my hard work.

"He left as soon as I was old enough to have my own place." This time, the tears do fall. His betrayal was harder to deal with than hers.

"I'm sorry. I didn't think he would leave."

It takes everything in me not to yell. I breathe, trying to get myself under control. On my way down, I'd promised myself I would be civil and kind. She's making it hard to do that and doesn't even seem to realize it. How can she berate him for leaving me when *she* left me first?

The doors open and I march out. She sticks to my heels, desperate to make me understand. Her pace slows as she realizes this is the same hall we lived in as a family. I draw up to the door and unlock it.

"You still live here?" She sounds shocked.

"Just because everyone else left, doesn't mean this isn't still my home."

We step inside and I'm transported to my childhood when I used to beg my mother to explore the Spire with me. Sometimes, we would walk for what felt like hours, looking at art, listening to music, and picking up snacks. Those used to be some of my favorite memories. Now,

I've blocked most memories of her out. They're easier to ignore than go through.

This feels like coming home to a place that no longer exists—a place a part of me desperately wishes had stayed in one piece. I've emerged from the pieces as the person I am today, and while it was a hard road, I am grateful for where I've ended up. She can't come back and expect to fill in the role of my mother. Not when that role doesn't feel necessary anymore.

"Can I get you something? I have some drinks and there's leftovers." The kitchen is cleaner than I expected. The dishes are stacked on a drying rack, water droplets running down them. The food must be inside my fridge.

"Did I interrupt something?" she asks.

"Like it or not, no matter when you showed up, it would be an interruption. But yes, I was having supper with some friends." I intentionally stab her with my words.

She stiffens, then lifts her face with bravery. "I would like to meet your friends."

"Why?" I feel like a teen again. This sullen need to contradict and inflict pain is so juvenile. Freeing the bitter thoughts brings me a lot of satisfaction. I start putting the dishes away, desperate for a distraction.

"Because I came here to make sure you're okay."

I freeze and the dish in my hand almost slips out. I set it down, a little too hard, and look at the ceiling. "I'm fine. In fact, over the past few weeks my life has been great. I'm happier than I've ever been, and I think I finally know what I'm doing. There. Does that answer your question?" When I look at her, she's staring at the paintings. They're lying on the table. She looks carefully at the portrait.

"Don't touch that. It's delicate." I hurry over and pick it up. I don't want her to see *this* part of my life.

"Who made this?"

"My friend Alix. He was here tonight." I'm already heading toward my bedroom to put it back on the wall. I leave my own paintings behind. I hardly care what she thinks of them. It's this one that feels too private.

"Does he love you?"

Another wave of frustration washes over me. "We're just friends, okay? I only met him recently."

"His painting carries traces of love. I'm good at reading people."

I bite my tongue. It is not her place to tell me who does and doesn't love me. I hang the painting back on the wall. She has followed me into the bedroom, which used to belong to her and my father. It is no longer her space and I silently dare her to challenge me for it.

She just looks around, seeming lost in a place she thought would be familiar.

"I can't do this tonight. Can we just ... put this all on pause and start again tomorrow? I need to sleep."

She backs out of the room. "I'll take the couch."

I don't care where she sleeps. She could lie on the floor, and it wouldn't bother me. I close the door behind her, barely making it into my bed before the sobs start erupting. I hug my pillow, determined not to let her hear me. I don't want her to know how much it breaks me to see her. I want so desperately to sink into her arms and feel loved, but I've built a barrier between us in my mind, and it seems impossible to break down.

In just one night, I feel sent back to square one, overwhelmed with emotions and trapped in my own house. I sit up, realizing I can do whatever I want. My mother being here doesn't mean I can't do things the way I normally would if she were gone.

I want to begin to understand her side. It's the only way for us to move forward. As much as I don't expect us to ever be close, I would like us to be on better terms when we part again. I need to go up to the roof. I need to think before I speak to her again.

When I step out, my mother is in the kitchen. She watches as I cross the room and step out. Neither of us speak, but I hope she finds the peace in my absence that I'm hoping to find in hers. A wall is not enough to separate us right now. I need more. *We* need more.

So I travel up the few floors to the roof and step out beneath the infinite sky.

THIRTEEN

I stand still for a couple minutes, simply breathing in the night air. My comm buzzes with a notification: Lekka asking what happened. When I tell her my mother came, she asks if I'll be helping with the garden tomorrow morning. I say I will. If there's anything I need right now, it's my early morning shifts.

I put on the harness and walk to the edge of the building. I don't sit, choosing instead to lean out and test the wind. The rope pulls taut behind me. The arches of my feet rock back and forth as I face the ground so far below.

I consider jumping when a hand grabs my shoulder and pulls me back. I gasp, stumbling and falling onto my back. When I look up, Lekka is staring down at me. Her eyes narrow as she judges my condition.

"I figured I should check up here to see if

you're okay. Good thing I did."

I scramble to my feet. "I'm fine."

"*Fine* is being downstairs with your mother who you haven't seen for years. Jumping off a building without any training is *not* fine." She shakes her head, frustration building across her face. "Maybe I've been a little lax with my training, but you can't do things like that without me here. I've had years to practice and even I shouldn't do those things on my own."

"I'm sorry," I whisper, my heart dropping into my stomach. I've never seen her like this. It scares me. Are things going to change between us? So far, our relationship in and out of work has transitioned back and forth easily, but I fear she has lost trust in me and won't risk my safety on account of being friends.

"Not as sorry as I'd be if your body was found on the sand tomorrow. That would kill me. If you're going to jump, you're going to do it right." She heads on over to the shed and starts putting on her own gear. I watch her tighten and shift, working her way into the straps until she feels secure. Then she begins checking my own harness, her quick fingers making a few adjustments.

"Rule one"—she walks backwards, stopping when she's in front of me—"is that you never do this while angry. This is not supposed to be that sort of outlet. It's too dangerous for that."

I nod. "I'm not angry. I just wanted to clear my mind."

"Clearing your mind is going for a walk around the Spire, not jumping off the top. This is pure, risky fun. Got it? You're not allowed to do this alone and you're not allowed to do it when I feel you're not stable enough."

I shift. If she'd heard me earlier, would she still let me do this?

"I know your day has been rough, but I expect you to put that aside before we do this. I'm trusting you to tell me if you don't feel ready for this."

"I'm fine. Really."

She eyes me with distrust.

"If you didn't think I'm ready, you wouldn't be willing to let me do it."

Her face softens. "I know you need a friend right now, not a mentor. I will do my best to be both. Don't make me regret this." She leads me to the edge. "The ropes are built to stop us from falling. When you jump, you'll free fall for a couple seconds before it starts to slow down. From the very top, a good jump will get you about forty stories down."

I toe the edge, ready to get going. I want to feel the wind in my hair and the emptiness beneath my body.

"Hold on a second. You have to listen to me." She sticks out her arm and pushes me back a little. "We're going to jump at the same time. We'll be holding hands so the wind doesn't crash us into each other. That means when I count down, you have to jump with me. If I jump and you don't, we'll spiral into an uncontrolled fall."

"Okay." I can't seem to catch my breath. This is so frightening, yet so exciting.

"Okay, now look down."

I do, taking in the gardens stretching between us and the ground.

"Where should we jump?"

There are two options: the first being where we walk down to garden, the second being the space between the separate gardens. While there's a line cutting between each garden for the gardener, there's an even wider space that allows the gardens to be marked in different sectors. It's enough space for me and Lekka to shoot through.

I point at it.

"Perfect. You pass that test." She laughs.

I hold out my hand and she takes it. "I'm ready." I reassure myself with those words. It's the same as drowning out any other emotion: I just push the fear down and don't let it take over.

She holds on tight. The countdown begins.

One,

Two,

Three.

We jump. I launch myself off while she does more of a careful jump and we fall into the great nothingness. A scream escapes my throat—one of thrill and exhilaration. The weightlessness filling my body is a burning feeling. I never want to let it go.

The first layer of gardens flies past, then the second. I wonder if people are watching us fall past their windows. I try to keep my eyes open, but the wind makes them water and I have to blink. I don't want to miss a moment of our insane descent. The rope begins to tighten as we slow from the fall. I stretch my free arm out and whoop.

We come to a stop almost halfway down

the Spire. I tip my head back and drink in the wind whistling around us. It's intoxicating, screaming of a sort of freedom I have never felt before.

I am a bird taking its first flight.

I am a ship preparing to leave orbit.

I am a daughter who has a chance to know her mother.

All of this unfolds inside of me. I look at Lekka. "Thank you."

"I didn't do anything. You took the leap."

My heart soars. I did take the leap and I will continue to do it again and again. Even though my mother has come back, disrupting the new life I'm enjoying, I can't let that drag me back down. I have to find a way to climb out of this cycle of hating her and needing her. I *will* find a way.

"Are you okay?" Lekka watches me closely. Her hand is still tight in mine. We're rising now, the ropes spooling back in. When there's an uncontrolled fall, they're programmed to begin pulling up as soon as the fall is broken. It's going to take us a couple minutes to reach the top.

"I just don't know where to go from here. I have a stranger in my house, one I'm supposed to be close to. It's hard to come to terms with."

"Then don't."

"What?"

She shrugs. "The way I see it, she gave away all rights to your kindness when she walked out. You don't have to accept her again."

"But I don't feel right closing her out. No matter how much space I put between us, there's something binding us together."

"Then you need to make her understand who you are now and what you need from her. Don't hide things, let it all out. The least she can do is listen."

I think about that. It's true. Over the years, I needed her to be there for me. I needed someone who would understand a bit of what it meant to be me. Even if she wasn't, she at least owed it to me to listen. "I just want her to see that I care about her, but ... don't need her back here. I want her to know that she can go back to the desert and not think about me again if that's what she wants."

Lekka squeezes my hand. "Are you really okay with her disappearing again?"

"Doesn't matter what I want, she'll do it anyway." I know she needs the desert. I feel a pull to the desert, one that comes from all the parts of me that are spyren. Her entire body feels that call to the purple sand. It would be cruel for me to deny her that. "Do you mind if I bring my mother gardening sometime? I want her to see what I'm doing now that I've stopped reading memories."

"Bring her. Just don't fight when you're out here," she jokes.

"Don't worry. We won't." I smile. "I don't know if I've quite forgiven her, but I want her to see my life. I want her to understand that I'm okay. I think that's what she's here for."

It stings, knowing she came just to clear her guilty conscience, but clearing the air will make the future easier for both of us. No more what-ifs or maybes, just the solid truth. There is a faint tie between us now, a remnant of our mother-daughter connection, but it's time to cut it and set ourselves free.

"She must've missed you."

"Maybe, but I don't know if she came for me or my dad. She didn't know he moved out."

Lekka grabs my harness and pulls me in, giving me a tight hug. I grip her tightly and bury my face in her shoulder. "Don't forget that some families are chosen. If you need someone to consider family, I'm always around. I can be your older sister, if you'd like, or some crazy aunt who never leaves you alone."

I snort, then pull in a shaking breath. "Thank you for that. I would be honored to call you family."

We stay close until the edge of the roof comes in reach. I grab it with my hands and pull myself up. My muscles burn, but less than they did the first time. When I stand, I feel I have found my footing in more ways than one.

FOURTEEN

I sneak in that night, then sneak out the next morning.

Both times, my mother is asleep on the couch. She doesn't rustle, not even when I make myself a warm cup of coffee. Tiptoeing around my own home is a strange feeling. I feel invasive.

Yesterday's events have been on replay in my mind. One of the best days of my life turning into one of the most complicated nights is not what I had in mind when I'd invited Lekka over. I know the complicatedness is waiting for me when I return. By then, Mother will be awake and ready to talk.

I just need to know what to say.

Lekka doesn't speak much while gardening. We meet, get ready, and start down. It's become almost routine for me. I work my way around the plants, spritzing as I go, the soil familiar between my fingers.

In my head, I rehearse what I'll say when I get home. I need to sit down with my mother and have a conversation about yesterday. I feel guilty for the way I treated her. I don't want the guilt, but I also don't think an apology is what we need. We need to talk like adults and speak about our mistakes in a mature manner. I can no longer treat her like she's nothing.

Somewhere deep inside me is a little girl who has been waiting for her mother to come home.

Lekka comes up beside me when I reach the panels. "It's harvesting day for some of these," she says. She hands me a net to loop in my belt. "Pick the ones that feel soft. If they're hard, they're not quite ready."

Because the gardens are grown in alternating cycles, the harvest takes place at different times. Though usually the later shifts do the bulk of the harvesting, Lekka and I still gather what we can.

I dig my hands in, coated with the nutrients, and work my way across the panel. I enjoy the feeling of adding the nutrients. It's warm and gooey on the gloves and each time I pull away, I'm coated in the rich soil.

I squeeze the tubercles as I go; some are hard as rocks while others give way beneath the pressure. I pull those out, the indents of my fingers present on their soft skin, and fill the bag.

The sun seems to rise faster today, my forehead and the back of my neck are coated in sweat. I wipe it out of my eyes. My talk with my mother is going to have to wait until I've showered.

Lekka appears when I've finished my second panel. "If you need to leave early, feel free. I can do the last ones by myself."

"Are you sure?"

"I've been doing this on my own for a while, I think I'll manage. Go on now." She hands me a couple bags of tubercles to bring up with me. I add them to my belt and start the climb back to the top.

I drop the harvested tubercles in a bin by the elevator. Once the first shift is done, someone will come up to collect the food. I work my way out of the harness. It's time for me to begin the hardest part of the day.

◊◊◊

Breakfast waits on the table when I get out of the shower. She's already eaten and is washing up a few dishes. I stand in the doorway without announcing my presence. This is such a normal scene, a daughter watching her mother, and I want it to last for a moment longer.

"I know you're there," she says.

I walk into the kitchen and take a seat. She's warmed up some of the leftovers from yesterday. It's not what I would've eaten for breakfast, but I appreciate the gesture.

"Where do you go in the mornings?"

"I'm a gardener. I work an early shift."

Her hands stop scrubbing for a moment. "You don't read memories for people anymore?"

I pause, food almost in my mouth. "How do you know I read memories?"

"I didn't completely disappear. I had someone watch you until I thought you were going to be okay."

I sigh, setting the food down. "When did you think I was okay?"

"When you started connecting with the

desert. I assumed that would straighten you out. It would care for you like it has for me."

"It ended up breaking me. I can't process memories properly."

"I worried about that, you know. I never meant to have a child with a human. I knew there was a big risk." She leaves the sink and takes a seat across from me.

"I didn't know what to do. The desert rejected me, so I've poured myself into the Spire."

She holds out her hands and I take them. "I am sorry you went through that alone. I ... should've better prepared you to deal with being half spyren. I was scared to broach the topic. I told myself I didn't know any more than you did, but of course I did. You were never introduced to your culture properly and it left you confused."

She was put in an unfair position just like me. She came here for love but had to choose her health over it. I know why she left. Her need to enter the desert must be as strong as my need to leave it. In that way, we still have a bit of a connection between us.

"I'm sorry for everything I said yesterday. It wasn't fair of me," I start, somehow falling into the very apology I swore I'd avoid.

"I shouldn't have shown up like that." She leans back in her chair and shakes her head. "I just had to see you again. Once I leave here, I'm going to try to find your father. I have things I need to say."

"Why now?"

She leans back, her hands slipping from mine. "Because I think I'm dying."

Nothing could've prepared me for that. I look at her, my mouth open, the entirety of my world crashing around me. "Why?"

"My body's failing. I can't read memories as well. I'm struggling to breathe, and I can feel myself slipping in many ways. I didn't think I'd make it this far, but the need to speak to you and your father kept me going. I'll have to see if I can hold out long enough to find him."

"We can get you in to see doctors. I'm sure they can fix this."

She holds up her hand, her face tired. It only hits me now just *how* tired she looks. While I've been blatantly berating her, she's been silently dying. The shame filling me turns my stomach. "I don't want to see a doctor."

"Why not?"

"Because it is the spyren way to die when

it's your time. I don't want half my body to be mechanical in order for it to run. That's not living. That's existing. Treatment would keep me in the Spires. I'd rather die in the desert than battle for life in here."

"But ..."

"I already lost so much of my life in the desert when I was with your father. Don't ask me to do this. I've said goodbye to all this." She gestures at everything around us.

"When do you want to leave?"

"When it feels right. I don't want to die with you angry at me."

I slip out of my chair and close the distance between us, kneeling on the ground and hugging her small body. She strokes my hair and whispers a forgotten lullaby in my ear. It took a lot of strength for her to come back. I respect her for it. She could've died without a word, leaving me to wonder about her.

This way, I'll know. It will be closure.

Still, now that she's in my arms, I can't bear the thought of letting her go.

"I'm not angry at you. Not anymore."

"Good." Her hands slow and she rests

them on my shoulders. I tilt my head up and look at her. "I'm proud of you and what you've become. If being away from the desert means peace for you, then I want you to follow the next best thing."

I sniffle, tears clouding my eyes. "Can I show you the next best thing?"

She pauses. "You want me to go gardening with you?"

"Yeah. I want you to see the thing that makes me as happy as the desert makes you."

She looks out the window, probably picturing the gardeners hanging on their ropes.

"You don't have to if it scares you."

She scoffs. "If I'm dying, fear is not something to consider. I would like to see this part of you. I probably should leave tomorrow anyways. Now that I've spoken to you, I need to try to make amends with your father."

I consider going with her, but I quickly dismiss that thought. I have no desire to face him again, and crossing the desert in my state would be exhausting.

Instead, I hold her tight while she's here, and hope these few hours make up for years of lost memories.

FIFTEEN

It's early and the wind is fierce. My mother's hand is tight in mine as Lekka works on fitting her into a harness. I squeeze, trying to reassure her through touch. We've spoken very little today, as if we've said everything we need to and are now content to be in each other's presence until she leaves. I've felt numb since our conversation yesterday. The bitter cold is enough to snap me out of it.

I can't quite process that she's going to be leaving this afternoon. When she disappears, I will likely never see her again. She will continue her search for my father and meet him or die trying. Either way, she'll die soon, and the desert will take her home.

Lekka hasn't spoken much to her beyond the introduction. It's easy to tell she's trying to do her job while also not interrupting anything between me and my mother. I'll have to thank her later; I owe her a lot for this.

"I don't love this wind," Lekka comments. It's flying around us like an angry beast.

I have to agree. It's making me nervous. "How often does it get this windy?"

"Often enough, but it still bothers me. We should be fine. Just be ready to come back up at any time." She's making an effort to look brave, but I spot the worry in her expression.

"If my being here is a problem—" my mother begins.

"No, don't worry about it." Lekka takes her free hand gently. I messaged her yesterday about my mother's condition and she has been very careful while preparing her for the climb. "The wind blows whether you're out here or not. I'm going to do my best to take care of you."

I'm glad Lekka hasn't mentioned anything about us not going down. Showing my mother the gardens is the last thing I need to do with her. I want her to leave knowing I've found something that means as much to me as the desert does to her. It will help her to die in peace knowing I've found my place in the universe.

"We're going to work close together today. I just want us all to be careful," she says. "The work is going to go by quickly because we have more to do." When we first came out, she told us that once we finish tending them, we'll have to cover the gardens to protect them against the wind.

"Sounds good."

Lekka straps us together with a rope, making sure my mother is between us since she's the one without any experience. With each other as support, we step to the edge and start tilting back.

Lekka runs through some quick rules as we begin a careful descent. With my mother between us, the risk of anything happening to her is low. We stick close to the wall as we approach the first garden.

I hand my mother the water and she starts spraying, while Lekka and I look for diseases. In the days I've worked here, I've never found anything bad on a leaf. I wonder how often those things happen.

More gardeners are coming down. One of them stops to talk to Lekka before continuing down lower. I can't hear the conversation due to the wind, but Lekka turns to me. "He's going to do our panels. A bunch of the gardeners are coming to help make today short."

By the time we're done, other gardeners have dropped down around us. They hand Lekka the folded covers that wrap around the gardens. She unfolds one, the wind loud within its domed top, and we fit it over the garden, the bottom clipping to the pot.

"This is fun," my mom says, her eyes alive.

"This isn't how it normally is, but yes ... it is fun." I wanted a normal experience, but I'll take what I can get. If my mother's greatest takeaway is that I have a fun job, I'm happy with that.

We're already moving down to the next garden. Since the other gardeners are working below us, Lekka doesn't have to worry about splitting up to go and tend the lower panels. My mom picks up the job as quickly as I did. She's in tune with the natural world. Her hands know how to act around the plants.

The teamwork between the gardeners is like a beautiful dance. When I ask Lekka about it, shouting to be heard over the wind, she tells me that on days like today the gardeners only run one shift. It's too risky to do multiple.

Because the workers are excited to get most of the day off, an almost celebratory tone hangs in the air. I reckon many of them will go back to bed once this is done and sleep in for as long as they want.

When my mother leaves, I might try to find Alix. I haven't seen him since the night she arrived. I need to tell him about my mother and let him know I'm okay. He was worried when I left and I haven't had the time to reach out.

Thoughts of him start filling my head. I think about the way time passed while we made food together. I still don't know how I feel about him. My mother seems to think he loves me, but she's only judging based on a painting.

She reads memories, not paintings.

I do wonder if she noticed something I've missed.

I enjoy being around him, but I don't know if it's love. I'm scared to push our relationship forward because I'm scared of rejection or, even worse, a change in my emotions. I'm waiting for him to take the first step.

My mother grabs my arm and points out at the moon. Her eyes are wide with wonder as she looks at the world in a way she's never seen before. I follow her finger, my mouth falling open as I take in the thick clouds of purple sand rising in the distance. Aygysi has been swept up into a frenzy. It feels very raw up here, as if the moon itself is breathing.

A gardener climbs up beside us and talks to Lekka. She glances my way as they speak and my stomach sinks. Beneath us, I hear the tail-end of frantic yells. People are starting to climb.

"There's a sandstorm coming. We have to retreat," she orders.

A shudder runs through my body. Some of the sandstorms on Argysi are big enough to consume the Spires in thick clouds of sand. My mother senses my trepidation. She places a comforting hand on my wrist.

We start the climb, the ropes' pulleys and gears assisting us. It's harder with the three of us, my mother's inexperience holding us back. The wind keeps pulling at us. I turn to Lekka, then notice the air behind her. It rolls across the sandy moonscape like boiling water, racing toward us, toward me. It's a wall that's going to slam straight into us. A scream builds in my throat. Some of the other gardeners have spotted the stormfront and they hug the Spire. For them, it's a matter of not wanting the wind to blow them around.

For me, it's a matter of not wanting the sand to split my mind in a million different ways.

Lekka sees it and her shoulders sag in defeat. We won't reach the roof in time. Even if we did, we wouldn't get out of the harnesses before it hit. Taking action, she pulls us close to the wall and shows my mother how to put on her goggles, cover her face, and breathe through the oxygen tube. I spread my hands out and press my legs to the cool glass. I snap the goggles on, the rubber rims suctioning to my skin.

My mother's hand reaches mine and she clasps it. "Share the memories," she shouts.

"What?"

Before she can answer, the storm hits.

The sand feels like teeth trying to break through skin. The memories are like knives on my soul. They're part of a great undoing, my very being unzipped before the power of the moon. The memories flood me without anywhere to put them. Sensations of every emotion burst through my pores. I scream, my mouth opening wider than feels possible. It's not just the pain of it all, it's the pressure of them building.

Just when I think they'll tear me apart, something loosens. Somehow, they've found a way to escape: a hole in the dam of my soul, a lifeline from me to my mother. I can't hold them any longer. The dam breaks. The torrent of memories fly from my hands and infiltrate my mother.

I feel hands on my back. Other climbers have come to help us up. Lekka is climbing, her loud voice occasionally cutting through the storm. The top of the Spire comes within reach. The memories are still flowing, but they're no longer trapped in me.

I help pull my mother up. She's limp in the harness, deadweight. Her mouth moves as she whispers something to the wind. The sand doesn't stop. It never stops. The harnesses are peeled from our bodies, and we're ushered inside.

The memories fade as soon as we're out of the storm. I lean against the wall, trying to catch my breath. My mother crumples on the floor.

"Mother?" I kneel beside her. She's so weak, so unable to fight against the world. Her breaths are quick and uneven.

"I should've never let you two come today." Lekka kneels on the other side.

It's not Lekka's fault. I pushed her into letting my mother come, wanting to do one last thing with her. I told Lekka the situation. It was unfair to put her in that position, knowing she should forbid us but also knowing it was our last chance to do this.

Lekka lifts my mother in a way I never could. I might be taller, but my arms aren't built of the same muscle. When we reach my home, I open the door to my bedroom and Lekka places my mother carefully on my bed. Sand falls into the sheets, drained of its memories. My mother hasn't opened her eyes yet. When I hold her wrist, I can feel her gentle pulse through her skin.

"Do we need to get a doctor?" Lekka asks.

"This isn't something that can be healed. It's a matter of the mind, not the body." I press my forehead against my mother's, wishing I could take back some of the memories. She did this for me, seeing the pain the memories caused and opening herself up to them.

I can't forgive myself for making her feel like she had to do that.

Lekka pulls a chair in and sits by the door while I wrap myself around my mother and comfort her with the same songs she sang to me as a child.

SIXTEEN

I brush sand from my mother's hair. She hasn't woken yet, has hardly stirred in the two hours I've been watching her. My hand rests on her chest as I feel for her breaths. An aching fear has opened within me that her breaths will suddenly stop, and I'll be unable to do anything about it.

The sun rose a long time ago, but the moon is dark. Outside, purple sand slices through the air, battering against the side of the Spire. I listen to the sound of the storm and curse my foolishness for taking my dying mother into it.

She would've been fine had it not been for me. I know she can control the amount of memories she takes in, but once they were in me, she was the only available place for them to drain.

Lekka sits in the corner. She's silent, scrolling through her comm. I appreciate the unspoken support.

"You don't have to stay," I say, turning to face her.

"I'm going to be right here if you need me." She closes her comm and crosses her legs. "Someone else is coming, too. I thought we could use some food."

Now that she mentions it, a devouring hunger grows in me. I try to ignore it, pain spiking through my stomach.

Someone knocks on the door. I glance at Lekka.

"Do you want me to get it?" She starts to get up.

"Sure." I slink back to the bed, checking to make sure Mother's okay. I hear Lekka in the other room as she speaks in hushed tones, explaining the situation to whoever's here. I peek through the door, hope building in my chest, and smile when I see Alix.

He stands by the table, already-made food in his hands. He looks up. "I'm so sorry, August," he says, smiling sadly.

I nod. I'm feeling a little numb to it all right now. He hands me some food and I take it. "Thank you. For everything." I sniffle. Tears build and I blink them away.

"Hey, of course. It was no problem." He gives me a hug. I sink against his body. It feels nice to have something living that feels so solid. I'm used to hugging the lifeless walls of the Spire, soaking in echoes of life that reverberate through them.

My mother makes a noise that sounds like a word and a groan. I drop the food on the table and run back to her side. Lekka and Alix follow, standing in the door.

She's awake. Her eyes take in the room. When they land on me, they fill with relief. "I thought I'd lost you," she whispers.

"I'm right here," I sob, grabbing her hands. "I will always be right here."

She leans back on the pillows. She's exhausted. Her body is strained, and she has no extra energy. "I need to move on. I need to see your father before it's too late." She speaks with urgency.

I look back at Lekka and Alix. "Are there any transports leaving here?"

They shake their heads. Transports between Spires don't happen often, maybe once or twice a month.

"I can't take a ship. I must walk there."

"But you'll die." I imagine her caught up in a storm like the one outside. She's in no condition to force herself through a harsh world when we have easier methods of traveling.

"I do not fear death. Why are you determined to fear it for me?" She reaches out to touch my face, wiping away the tears. "I will rest until the storm goes, and then I will be on my way. Alone. If the moon wills it, I will see your father again. If not, I will be dead, and it will hardly matter then."

Twinges of anger spark. She is stubborn and unwilling to see things from my point of view. If she would just visit a doctor, she could live for many more years. She could enjoy the moon, meet my father, and live with her people.

Instead, she is choosing to let her body shut down. I can't understand it. Perhaps it's because I've grown with humans who have cures for almost everything. Most people in the spires die of old age. My mother is too young for age to kill her.

"Just promise me one thing," she asks.

"Anything."

"Promise me you'll continue to be kind to yourself. You're too hard on yourself. You get angry when you don't meet your own expectations." She shakes her head at my so-called foolishness. "Rely on the people around you more. It's the only way to thrive." I nod, aware that Lekka and Alix are hearing these words too. She looks past me, inspecting them. "Is that the boy who painted you?" She asks.

I laugh, partly out of embarrassment and partly out of her calling him a boy. "Yes."

"He looks nice." She seems to be at peace with that as she closes her eyes and falls back asleep.

◊◊◊

Alix and Lekka stay with me at the table. I'm grateful for their companionship. I don't think I could do this on my own.

"Should I let my mother go?" I let the question hang between us.

"Your mother knows she's dying. All she wants is to set things right before she goes." Alix locks eyes with me. "I think it's best to let her do that on her own terms."

How am I supposed to let go of her? In

what world does a daughter knowingly let their mother die? I close my eyes and rest my face in my hands. Lekka places her hand on my left shoulder, her soothing voice telling me it's going to be okay.

But it's not. It might never be okay again.

I know I have to let her go.

She needs to approach her end in the way that feels right to her. I just think I was never enough of a priority for her. I wish she cared for me as much as she cared for the desert. If I'd filled such a spot in her life, she would've never left me behind.

I've forgiven her because there doesn't seem to be any other choice. I won't let her die without knowing I tried to put our past behind us. I wish I had more time to come to terms with it.

She could've died taking the memories from me. She was willing to give her life to take away my pain. But why did she have to wait until she was dying to offer herself to me?

I mourn more than her inevitable death. I mourn the fact that her death completely closes off all possibilities of a close bond between us. I spent so much time hating her, she spent so much time avoiding me, and now we're going to face a great divide.

It might've been easier if she'd never come back at all.

To grieve over what I might have had seems foolish, but it's a very real feeling.

Signed,

one who has to be complete on their own

SEVENTEEN

Her face is inches away from mine. I jerk back, a startled cry escaping. With her gaunt face, my mother looks like some sort of ghost. She apologizes as I sit up and try to calm my heart.

"What's going on? Why are you up?" When I'd fallen asleep on the couch, she was still resting in my bed.

"I need to leave now, but I couldn't leave without saying goodbye."

It takes me a moment to register her words. I look out at the dark desert. It's no longer storming. The sand lies calm across Argysi. Oviun hangs in the sky, an edge of the sun's light peeking around its horizon.

"It's way too late to leave. Can't you wait until morning?"

"I have to leave now. I ... if I don't, I fear I

never will."

I get off the couch and pull her in for a hug. Beneath my fingers, I feel her fading as surely as the sun sets at night. She would rather die in the desert than die in the Spire and I won't deny her that final wish. She will most likely not reach my father.

"Thank you for coming. You have no idea how much seeing you again meant to me."

She exhales softly. "Probably as much as it meant to me." Her frail hands rise to my shoulders. "You have a lot of good ahead of you. I can feel it."

Her words hold no certainty, but they bring me peace. I turn my head so she doesn't see the tears spilling down my cheeks. I was not built for goodbyes. It was easier the first time when she left without telling me. At least then I only had the anger to deal with. Now I feel like a failure.

We walk the Spire together. Her steps are slow, and I let her hold onto me. At this rate, I fear she will collapse before she even gets outside. On the elevator ride down, I watch her carefully.

"Are you sure about this?"

"More sure than I've ever been before." She brushes her hair back. She's still so beautiful.

"If you ever see him again, can you tell him that I meant to talk to him?"

She knows she won't reach him. She might have if it hadn't been for our mishap. I curse myself again for taking her to the gardens at such a horrible time. I have taken her final dream out of her hands and crushed it. She will never see the man she loved again.

"I will."

That promise binds us. When we get to the bay, it's empty. She's lucky I'm a sand reader; not everyone has access to open these doors. The Spire doesn't want anyone just wandering out into the desert.

I punch in the code and the door starts opening. It's large, cracking open at the top and lowering slowly as a ramp. A soft breeze sweeps in; it's better than anything I've ever smelled before. The desert is serene. It's the perfect place to die. Maybe one day, I'll stand here myself and prepare to hand my body over to the moon.

More likely, I'll die in the hospital surrounded by tubes and worried people.

I understand the need for more peace.

She gives me another hug. We don't speak, everything having already been said. Her small form starts down the ramp. When she arrived, she seemed more full of life. Maybe it was my fear building her up to be bigger than she was, but she filled this room with her presence. Within the last day, I've seen her withering away.

I stand in silence for ten minutes and watch her cross the desert with slow, determined steps. The wind picks up, sheets of purple sand filling the air. One moment she is there, the next she is gone, enveloped by the place she loves.

◊◊◊

When Oviun is high in the dark night sky, I find myself alone at the top of the Spire. Maybe I came up here to catch a final glimpse of my mother, but that moment has long passed behind the shifting sand.

Though I don't expect a response, I send a message to Alix, asking him if he's awake, asking if he'd join me on the roof.

Twenty minutes later, he says he's on his way.

I'm not standing at the edge. The harnesses are all hung up, the ropes are all in their places. I don't want to leave the roof tonight. I want to stay up here beneath the universe and shed the weight of existence.

I'm still the lost girl I was when my mother arrived, still searching for meaning on a strange moon, but perhaps I'm more prepared to follow the currents of life now that I've had a chance to say goodbye. Even if that doesn't make it hurt any less.

The door opens and Alix steps out. "Is something wrong?" he asks.

"My mother left tonight, and I was feeling alone." I pat the roof beside me. "I was hoping you wouldn't mind keeping me company."

He takes a seat beside me, his arm creeping around my shoulder. I lean against him. I'm doing my best not to cry.

On the way up here, I realized my mother has gotten the ending she wanted. When she dies, she will not cease existing; her final memories will be released into the sand for her people to find. I believe her soul will find its way somewhere else while the remains of her body here will be a testimony to her life.

It's a beautiful thing, the cycle of life.

It should not be interrupted.

"How do you feel?" His voice is so close to my ear it tickles when he speaks.

"I feel content. I know she did what she thought was right. I don't think that's something I should've tried to take away from her."

"She loved you a lot." He has me tight in his arms, the warmth from his body creeping beneath my skin.

"Mmhmm."

He rests his head against the top of mine. I don't know what will happen from here. In losing my mother, I've gained more of myself. I have answers to questions that will no longer keep me searching. It's the perfect opportunity to open myself up to the world around me.

I turn my head and Alix looks into my eyes. I lean in, waiting for him to respond. He bends down and we kiss. It's gentle and slow and when we part, nothing seems to have changed. But I think it has. For us, this is a world of difference.

Everything I've ever experienced has led to this moment, a moment that could lead to many more like it. The past is a certain thing. It has happened and cannot be changed, its ups and downs permanent steps behind us. But the future is something we can hold in our hands and shape. In Alix's eyes, I see a future where we face life together.

My mother's visit has changed the way I view my life. She gave up one love for another, then died while trying to gain control of her life again. I don't want my life to end with the future still unshaped in my palms. I want to pursue everything that brings me peace and joy.

I smile and rest my head on his shoulder again. Until the gardeners come, it's just us alone at the top of the moon. The purple sands continue their dance on wild winds and Arygsi continues to spin, oblivious to our struggles, immune to our decisions.

EPILOGUE

When I got the notice of the visitor, I was laying by the glass with Alix, my head in his lap. I had lifted my comm as we both read the alert. His body tensed beneath mine and when I looked up, his eyes had grown wide, his smile too hopeful.

I shook my head. I had known it wasn't my mother. She was long dead.

But who else then, other than my father?

When I had reached the bay and saw the spyren, I stopped for a minute. I'd never met a spyren other than my mother. It was so strange seeing someone who brought back memories of her yet wasn't her.

She smiled cautiously. "You're August?"

"I am." I had almost stuck out my hand, but then pulled back when I'd realized I didn't know the traditional spyren greeting. Much of their culture still remains a mystery to me. Much of my mother will never be understood.

"I followed your mother's memories here," she'd explained. "I came across her deathground and knew I had to come find you."

"Her ... deathground?" The word was unfamiliar on my tongue.

"It's a strange translation. In our language, we would call it her *lielspring*. It's the place where she died and left her memories."

Her words had been a soft punch to the gut. I'd always known my mother was dead, but hearing it spoken so plainly was almost too much to bear. Until then, I'd been holding out on some hope that she was still alive and well, happily living in the desert.

"I don't know what to say. I knew she'd died, but I never *really* knew."

The spyren nodded. "I'm sorry to be the one bringing the news. When I saw you in her memories, I had to explain to you the way she saw you. I think it's something you'd like to hear."

"Would you like to come up to my home?" I extended an invitation.

"What I have to give won't take long."

She reached out, asking for my hands. Her fingers had been warm on mine, her skin tough from desert-living, as she rubbed circles on the backs of my hands. "Your mother's memories were painted with her love and pride for you. When I saw that bond and felt the uncertainty that she had over whether or not you felt her love, I had to come and let you know."

"I knew she loved me. I just had a lot of hurt associated with her." I hadn't been able to keep the tears back any longer. All the silent weight I'd been carrying burst forth. I'd felt alone in my inner struggles over my mother and had spent a lot of time wondering if she was still alive, even though I knew. I *knew.* Too many of my thoughts had been spent on whether I'd properly forgiven her before death. Hearing that she was unsure of my love for her brought forth a lot of guilt.

"I know. And rightfully so. She failed many times as a mother and she carried that guilt with her into death." The spyren let go of my hands and bent down to pick up a bag I hadn't noticed before. She pulled out a small jar full of rich, purple sand. It had almost looked alive in the glass, shifting as she held it out. "This is a piece of her deathground. I want you to have it. When you feel the need, you can experience your mother's memories for closure."

She had placed it in my hands, closing my fingers around it. I cradled this final piece of my mother—one of the most precious things I've ever received.

The spyren went to the door and opened up the pad. "I happen to know you have the code to get out of here, sand reader."

"I'm not a sand reader anymore," I'd said, stepping up beside her.

"I know, but perhaps one day you will return to it."

"You're sure you want to leave so soon?" I punched in the code and the door began to open.

"I have done what I came to do. The rest is up to you."

The rest? I'd looked at the sand, trying to think of what it could tell me. I hadn't read sand since the sandstorm that weakened my mother. How fitting would it be to return to my roots by reading her memories?

The spyren left and I'd watched her disappear in the sweeping sand, wondering what memories danced across her skin. I never got her name, but her name was not important. She had come to offer much more than herself.

When I had stepped back into the apartment, Alix was waiting by the door.

He noticed me coming in alone and saw the tear tracks on my cheeks. His face melted with concern. "Who was it?" he asked, coming in close to hold me if needed.

"The spyren who came across my mother's memories. The ones she left when she died."

"Oh, August. I'm so sorry to hear that." He followed me to the kitchen. I set the jar down carefully on the table, then turned, and buried myself in him. The glass had been cold in my hands, just a thin layer between me and whatever memories my mother left behind. Alix's warmth was a welcome change.

"What's in the jar?"

I pulled back from the embrace, looking over at the jar. "It's sand from my mother's deathground. It holds a collection of her memories."

He reached out to touch it, then stopped himself. "Are you going to read them?"

I shook my head slowly. "I don't feel ready. I'm going to wait." I picked the jar back up, eager to place it somewhere other than the table. My mother's memories deserved more than that.

"You should wait until it feels right."

I walked to our bedroom. The wall above our bed was full of paintings. The largest canvas I'd done so far was a wide painting of my mother's silhouette as she disappeared into the desert. It had been a challenge to get right since it stemmed from such an important memory. As I had smeared the paint lightly across her dark form, it had given me a sense of the distance between us.

In some ways, a barrier would always stand between us, and now that she'd died, the chance to tear it down was gone. Even the memories in this jar could end up meaning nothing to me.

But they could also mean *everything*.

It was that possibility that led me to place the bottle on the shelf next to a vase of dried flowers and a picture of me, Alix, and Lekka. The shelf had become a home for all my trinkets that carried special memories—a place for me to visit when I needed to be reminded of how blessed I was.

"Are you going to be okay?" Alix watched me from the door.

"Yeah, I think I am." I looked out at the light fading across Argysi. "We should go get something to eat."

"Agreed," he chuckled, extending his arm. When I took it, he pulled me close, giving me another firm hug. "I love you so much. I hope you know that."

"You only say it a million times a day." I broke from his hug and gave him a quick kiss. Living with someone who loved me and made sure to constantly tell me had helped me open myself up to the world. I was so lucky to have someone by my side who had never given up on me.

We left our home arm in arm and headed to the bustling core of the Spire, just two people on a purple moon in the center of an ever-expanding universe.

LETTER TO THE READERS

Dear Reader,

When my publisher suggested a letter about Moon Soul, I was overwhelmed with all the things I wanted to say. The truth is, having a letter in Moon Soul feels fitting since Moon Soul is, at its core, a letter to myself. Of course, it's a long and rather plotty letter, but a letter, nonetheless. I wrote it during a time in my life when I felt very lost. Not in who I was, (because I've always been very sure of who I am) but in where I was going.

Life is a strange thing. You 'grow up' and graduate only to realize that life has hardly begun, and it's actually the hard stuff that's ahead. I took a year off, decided on a college program, and now I'm here (two years later) finishing up college with no idea of where I'm going.

And then I wrote Moon Soul.

Moon Soul is ... *so many things.* It's a science fiction novella, it's a personal story, it's a character study, it's a fever dream. I wrote the rough draft in four days. In true Nathaniel nature, I looked at my two weeks break from work and decided not to work on this until I had four days left. At that point, it was a 'write it all now or never finish it' type of situation. I knew this was a story that had to be finished.

After spending thousands of dollars on college, you'd hope I'd be excited about graduating. The truth is, *this* is what's exciting. This writing and publishing and dreaming I've been doing. For that, I have to thank Dragon Bone Publishing. This isn't an acknowledgment section, but I have to thank the driving force behind this story. Dragon Bone Publishing (and by extension Effie Joe Stock) was such a lifeline for my creativity. I had a company/person who believed in me. Suddenly, every idea was worth pursuing because someone was backing me up.

Having been a writer for years, and having published for years, this was the first time I felt important. My work was actually part of a vision. I *wanted* people to read it. Until Moon Soul, I've always viewed writing as very personal because it comes from such a personal place. With Moon Soul, I just wanted it out of my hands and in the hands of the people who need it. I believe Moon Soul is an important story.

Moon Soul's main conflict mostly stemmed from my own frustration with work. I think work is important, and I'm very grateful to have the job I have. That said, there are days I come home and never want to go back. I find the concept of work to be draining since I'm expected to pour myself into a company I really don't view as significant in my life. I think it's especially hard for me because I already have a dream and a 'job' which brings me so much joy.

What's that job?

Being an author!

Hence the 'job' part of it, since I've been told many times, being an author isn't a real job. It is, and I know it is, but that doesn't change that it's not sustainable for the majority of authors. We're juggling writing and our 'real' jobs and whatever else life throws at us.

So Moon Soul was therapeutic. August is a character who deals with the same frustrations as me and pouring that onto the page felt so good. It also made me feel seen and understood when early readers identified with August.

But life throws us more than just the challenges at work; it also presents us with challenges from home. Which is why I spent so much time curating August's relationships.

The romantic relationship in Moon Soul was a new, unexpected challenge for me. Alix was actually added a little unexpectedly. He just worked his way in, and I fleshed him out and added some chapters in my rewrite to really give him his moment. Love is not something I'm personally currently looking for, but it felt right for August to look for it. I gave her a very complicated home life because I wanted to give her more things to search for and an emptiness to fill, if you will.

Lekka was always the plan. She's an amazing friend and guide and someone full of wise advice. She's the type of friend I would treasure, and I wanted to give that to August.

I think the balance of Alix and Lekka ended up being perfect. August had different needs and they both helped her in different ways. I was able to throw in a lot of random friend anxiety and the feeling of not being enough—more personal stuff I wanted to see on page.

And of course, the last thing is August's

relationship with her mom and dad. I have two amazing parents and don't lack in that department at all, but I've always enjoyed exploring parental relationships in books, so I gave August a chance to deal with her mom.

That recognition of understanding without forgiving, but also building on a mutual understanding to reach a point of forgiving, was very important to me. I am a strong believer in people setting boundaries for their own health. August adjusting her boundaries as she got to know her mom was such a beautiful thing to me.

I won't lie and say I didn't cry while writing Moon Soul, because I definitely did.

While August didn't meet her father in the story, I would like to believe that eventually she sought him out. Maybe they even read her mother's memories together. Wouldn't that be beautiful? Or is it a little too 'happy ending' in a story that's already quite mushy and happy?

Either way, the Moon Soul universe is precious to me, and I am beyond excited that people are reading it. If you read to the end of this letter, I have to tell you that you mean the world to me. Taking a chance on my book is one of the kindest things you could do. Whether or not you enjoyed it is irrelevant, as I wrote this story to be read by everyone, even though I know it's bound to resonate more with some than others.

As Lekka would say, "Write what you want and don't let other people's opinions limit you."

And of course she would say that, because she's my character so she says whatever I tell her to say.

Before I risk building a god complex, I'll let you go. I hope to have many more stories to share with you in the future. Writing is, after all, my true job and I intend to take it as seriously as August does her gardening.

Wishing you all the great and beautiful things,

—Nathaniel Luscombe

ACKNOWLEDGEMENTS

There were a lot of people involved in various ways throughout the creation of this story.

I have to thank Kaitlynn for letting me sit in her rocking chair and tell her about Moon Soul while she played Roblox. I talked through the initial outline and gushed about each chapter I wrote, and she was clearly listening because my plot twists didn't surprise her.

I have to thank Sarah, Rebecca, and Oma for reading it and telling me that it was a story worth publishing.

Effie for reading it while I was in the hospital and telling me she'd publish it even if I died. This was very important to me. (Don't worry. I'm in good health.)

Dragon Bone Publishing for taking me on as an author. I constantly feel unworthy of all the cool things they do for me.

Everyone in my life who asks me for author updates and says they're excited for me.

And of course, all the authors who have ever written books that inspired me. I don't think Moon Soul would exist if it weren't for you. The best part of storytelling is acknowledging the fact that without storytellers ahead of me to inspire me, I don't know if I'd even be here right now. We're all just people living on one planet telling one continuous story.

I'm proud of Moon Soul for being part of that eternal chain.

www.ingramcontent.com/pod-product-compliance
Lightning Source LLC
Chambersburg PA
CBHW011336010826
48972CB00015B/2858
9781962337908